D1471769

Andrew Puckett worked in the NHS for twenty-one years, fifteen of them as microbiologist for the Oxford Blood Transfusion Centre, before turning to writing and teaching.

PRAISE FOR ANDREW PUCKETT:

'If medical mysteries are what keep you glued to your fireside chair . . . then look no further. Puckett, something of a master of the genre, has penned a cracker' – *Western Daily Press*

'A thoroughly well-worked mystery' – *Oxford Times*

'An interesting story with a very plausible plot and frightening overtones' – *Mystery News*

'A terrifying scenario made all the more chillingly believable by its similarities to real life situations' – *The Southern Daily Echo*

'The best thing about it is its remarkable feeling of authenticity' – *Birmingham Post*

SISTERS OF MERCY

ANDREW PUCKETT

ENDEAVOURINK

AN ENDEAVOUR INK PAPERBACK

First published by Andrew Puckett in 2014

This paperback edition published in 2017
by Endeavour Ink
Endeavour Ink is an imprint of Endeavour Press Ltd
Endeavour Press, 85-87 Borough High Street,
London, SE1 1NH

ISBN 978-1-911445-35-7

Typeset by Palimpsest Book Production Ltd, Falkirk, Stirlingshire

Printed and bound in Great Britain by
Clays Ltd, St Ives plc

www.endeavourpress.com

For the siblings,
Harriette Mullins
and
Christopher Puckett

Table of Contents

Chapter 1

'It's Mr Peters — I think he's dead . . .' Student Nurse Armitage looked breathlessly from myself to Mary . . . then we were moving across the ward as fast as we could without actually running.

'Screens,' Mary said to Armitage as she hit the alarm at the end of the bed, and Armitage drew the curtains around us.

Mary had stripped away his pyjama jacket and I reconnected him to the monitors, although I already knew we were too late. There's something about a dead person's face; not just the slackness of mouth and jaw, but the way the eyes are focused on to something not of this world . . .

I started external massage on his heart, putting all my weight on to the heels of my hands on his chest . . . I was briefly aware of the arrival of the crash team, then felt hands on my shoulders and a voice said in my ear, 'I'll take over now, Jo.' Stephen Wall, our senior registrar.

I stepped back.

The other members of the team were crowded round the foot of the bed with their equipment: James and Emma, staff nurses, and Graham Wood, the anaesthetist.

Stephen looked up at the cardiac monitor. 'Ventricular fibrillation,' he said. 'Intubate and oxygen, please, Graham,' then, 'Jump leads, please,' to Emma, who bought them forwards.

Jump leads is an example of the rather black humour we have to adopt in the Intensive Therapy Unit if we're to stay sane. Their proper name is defibrillator paddles and they're electric terminals which, applied to the chest over the patient's heart, causes them to jerk and, with luck, restarts the heart.

I knew that that wasn't going to happen this time, though.

And it wasn't just a sense of the macabre that sent a frisson through me as I watched Peters's body forlornly twitching.

Peters shouldn't have died.

He made the seventh patient to die of heart failure when they shouldn't, and now I was going to have to do something about it . . .

Mary said in my ear, 'You're wanted on the phone, Jo. We're OK here if you want to answer it.'

I thanked her and hurried back to the nurses' station where Armitage was holding it out for me.

'Sister Farewell, ITU.'

'Good morning, Sister. Miss Whittington here.' Miss Ann Whittington, nursing officer and my boss.

'Good morning, Miss Whittington.'

'I'd like to speak to you some time this morning, Sister, if that's possible.'

'Er — yes.' I glanced up at the clock. 'Would twelve o'clock be all right? There was something I wanted to speak to you about as well,' I added before I could change my mind.

'Very well, Sister. Twelve o'clock.'

I put the phone down slowly, aware that I'd committed myself to an action I dreaded.

Better prepare for it.

I de-gowned in the air-lock before going back through the Duty Room to my office and closing the door. I took a breath, tapped my password into the computer and found Peters's record.

Frederick Peters, age 49, married, two children . . . Address . . . Religion: Agnostic. Donor card: Yes. Tissue type . . .

My eyes flicked down . . .

Admitted on Monday with myocardial infarction but had responded well to isosorbide mononitrate therapy, and had had no further heart attacks. He'd been due to transfer to the Coronary Care ward tomorrow . . .

In other words, he shouldn't have died, not of heart

failure. It was why he'd been taken off the monitors, because he'd recovered so well . . . which is why we now didn't know exactly when he *had* died . . .

I printed out copies for Stephen and myself, then noted down the pertinent facts and added them to the six files I already had. I was still analysing them statistically with the calculator half an hour later when there was a tap on my door. I covered them with the second Peters printout as Mary came in. She shook her head briefly, then looked down at the printout on my desk.

'Anticipating events slightly, weren't you, Jo?'

For a moment, as I looked at her classically moulded face with its cornflower-blue eyes and tawny blonde hair, I was overwhelmingly tempted to confide in her . . . then I remembered that although she was my deputy and we got on well, I'd only known her for a few months and she did have a slightly over-loose tongue . . .

'Not really. It was pretty obvious.'

'I suppose so,' she said, still looking at me.

I said, 'What time are you going to lunch today?'

'One.'

'Good. I've been summoned to the presence at twelve, so you can keep shop for me.'

'What does the Witless want you for this time? Done something you shouldn't?'

'That, I shall discover at twelve.'

When she'd gone, I locked the files away and sat for

a few minutes thinking about them. Then Stephen came into the Duty Room and I went out to meet him.

'It's no good,' he said tiredly.

'Are you putting him on life support?' I asked.

'Yes. James is setting it up now. Did he have a donor card?'

'Yes.' I handed him the printout.

'Hmm. Well, I'd better go and contact the next of kin, I suppose.' He heaved a sigh. It was not a job any of us relished. It was bad enough informing someone of a loved one's death, let alone having to ask for their organs, but Stephen was the most scrupulous registrar I'd ever worked with so far as organ transplant was concerned. He was also a dish: an athletic six feet with russet hair and blue eyes in a strongly sculpted, somehow very English face.

Many doctors found excuses for not asking for the organs, but not Stephen. As he would say himself, it can sometimes be a comfort to relatives, knowing that another life can be saved. But not always . . .

*

At exactly twelve o'clock, I walked into the anteroom of Miss Whittington's office. Her secretary said, 'She's expecting you, Sister, go straight in.'

I tapped on the door though, before pushing it open.

'Ah, Sister Farewell. Please have a seat.'

Her desk was positioned so that her back was to the

window — a psychological trick many people in positions of authority like to adopt.

'Now, I believe you said there was something you wanted to speak to me about?' she said.

'Yes, but it's a rather . . . delicate matter. Perhaps after you've . . .?'

'Very well, although what I have to say concerns a matter of some delicacy as well. However . . .' Her pale grey eyes met mine . . .

Pale grey seemed to be her colour — her hair was pale grey, although in crisp, permed curls. Sometimes, she even wore pale grey. She was tall, slim, ageless; her unmade-up face was unlined, not unattractive, and yet somehow sexless. She was unemotional, firm, curiously formal.

'I have become concerned recently about a certain . . . lack of gravitas that has become apparent in ITU,' she said in her clear, incisive voice.

'I'm sorry you should think that,' I said slowly, then decided to call her bluff. 'I'm not exactly sure I understand, Miss Whittington . . .'

'I think you do,' she said. 'It is not you who are giving me cause for concern, but your new deputy — Mary Tamworth.'

So that was it. I took a breath.

'I know Mary Tamworth can be high spirited sometimes, but she's an excellent nurse and —'

'I'm sure she is, but on a ward like ITU, certain types

6

of humour are unacceptable. I have had a number of complaints about her from the medical staff, which my own observations have confirmed. Yesterday, for instance, I heard her — in the presence of a student nurse — refer to the mortuary technician as the *bone collector*: a clear and offensive allusion to this hospital's transplant policy.'

I remembered it myself. I'd noticed that she'd come in and was behind Mary when she'd said it, and hoped she hadn't heard. The point Mary was making was that by the time all the useful organs had been taken from the body, there wasn't much left but bones. A gross exaggeration, obviously, but . . .

'I'm very sorry this has happened, Miss Whittington, although I'm surprised that any of the medical staff should have complained, since she always seems to get on very well with them . . .' I paused, hoping for some names, but when none were forthcoming, I continued, 'However, I do take your point, and I'll speak to her about it.'

'Good. I must add though, that I'd have hoped a nurse with your experience would have grasped this particular nettle a little sooner.'

That irritated me.

'I think it's only fair to say that Sister Tamworth has had overall a good effect on ITU since she's been there. Her high spirits and her humour cheer up patients who have a lot to be worried about.'

Miss Whittington's lips tightened, although her voice remained light.

'Perhaps that is so, Sister, but you should know as well as anyone that a hospital depends on hierarchical respect for its efficiency: respect that is lacking in Sister Tamworth.'

So the crack about the bone collector wasn't all she'd heard.

'As I said, Miss Whittington, I do take your point and I will speak to her about it.'

'Good,' she repeated. 'That's an end to the matter.' She leaned back. 'Now, what was it you wanted to speak to me about?'

I hesitated, wondering whether to leave it after this worst of possible starts . . . No, it had to be done now . . .

'A delicate matter, you said,' she prompted.

'Yes.' I took a breath. 'Mr Peters, the MI who came in on Monday, died this morning. Cardiac arrest. He was due to transfer to Coronary Care tomorrow and we'd taken him off the monitors.'

'You're saying that you don't know exactly when the fatal attack occurred?'

'Yes, but that's not —'

'Potentially embarrassing, but it does happen. Write me a full report as soon as you can, please, Sister.'

'Of course, but that's only part of the problem. He *shouldn't* have died, Miss Whittington.'

'No, but patients sometimes do. I don't think any blame will attach to you.'

'That's not quite what I meant.' I searched for words. 'Miss Whittington, didn't you — *don't* you find that your experience will often tell you which patients are going to live; which to die?'

She looked at me a moment before replying.

'Yes. I think all good nurses have that facility to an extent. But it can be wrong. I assume you felt that Mr Peters would live?'

'Yes, I did, but —'

'You must know that in our profession we cannot afford to be sentimental, either with the patients, or with ourselves.'

'Miss Whittington, Mr Peters was the seventh patient in the last six weeks who was either in — or had just left — ITU, to have died when I was certain that they would live.'

She looked at me for longer this time.

'What exactly are you trying to say, Sister?'

'That I think we may have a serial killer in this hospital.'

*

Why does she stare at me so, I wondered. I found myself staring back, mesmerized, for some reason comparing our appearances . . .

I'm not beautiful like Mary, or a sexpot like Emma.

Or plain, that most dreadful of words, like Helen Armitage.

Those who like me say that my face is elfin; those who don't, say it is pointed. I have dark brown curling hair (worn up when on duty), hazel eyes and a clear skin. A good, although not sensational, figure. I don't have to worry about men any more, although I did at one time. Girls at school used to make jokes about my surname, said it was what my boyfriends were always saying to me . . .

'Sister Farewell,' Miss Whittington cut into my reverie, 'I have thought of you as one of the better nurses we have trained in St Chad's. It seems a shame that you should spoil that impression in so whimsical a way.'

'I assure you this is no whim,' I said. 'I have here' — I held up the files I'd brought with me — 'the details of all these patients. Perhaps, if we could go through them together, you will understand my anxiety.'

'Very well.'

I took the files out.

'The first is Mr Hanbury, nearly six weeks ago . . .'

Paul Hanbury, aged twenty — road traffic accident. It had been a miracle he'd survived in the first place, but after surgical repairs had been made and he'd been transfused with enough blood, there had been no reason for him to die, especially not from heart failure . . .

John Thorpe, fifty-six — a myocardial infarction, like poor Peters, that had responded well to drug therapy.

An otherwise healthy, optimistic man with everything to live for. He had died, apparently from another heart attack, the day he'd moved out of ITU to the Coronary Care ward.

David Longford, forty-five — aortic aneurism repair. His death had seemed particularly hard. A man whose smile could light up the ward, he'd been unlucky enough to have an aneurism, doubly unlucky to die of heart failure after a successful operation.

Isaac Goldman, sixty-five, a heart bypass patient. The operation had been successful and he'd just transferred to Coronary Care when he'd died, from heart failure.

Anne Lawrence, fifty. She'd had a total hysterectomy and had gone into postoperative shock. After transfusion and drug therapy, she'd stabilized and had been about to return to the Gynae ward when she'd died, also of heart failure.

Henry Newton, sixty-six. He'd nearly died of pneumonia, but had made a complete recovery after antibiotic treatment. He'd been about to transfer to the Medical ward, when he'd died — once again, from heart failure.

And now, Mr Peters.

Miss Whittington had shown increasing signs of impatience as I related these cases.

'Is that all of them?' she asked when I'd finished.

'Yes, but I've also —'

'Four of these patients were postoperative, and you

know as well as I that postoperative shock can cause heart failure.'

'That's true, I know, but —'

'And that patients who have had one heart attack are likely to have others, even after we think they've stabilized.'

'I know that, but —'

'Sister Farewell, these things happen. Yes, there may have been a lot of deaths in a short time, but you will see that it evens up over a period.'

'I know that's true generally,' I said, 'but I don't believe it is in this case. We've had seven unexpected deaths in the last six weeks, making a total of twenty deaths altogether.' I handed her the sheet of paper with my statistical analysis. 'You can see the number of deaths we've had in the last eight six-week periods, which I've converted into percentages. I've worked out the standard deviation on the mean of them, and the ninety-five per cent confidence limits. You can see that the percentage of deaths we've had in the last six weeks falls outside these limits. In other words, they didn't happen by chance.'

'But, Sister, being outside ninety-five per cent confidence limits is the same as a one in twenty chance, isn't it? You know as well as I that that sort of coincidence occurs every day in a hospital.'

I tried to explain that ninety-five per cent confidence limits and a one in twenty chance are not the same thing, but my own poor grasp of statistics wasn't a help. At last she said, 'Is there any specific person you think is behind this, Sister?'

'No, there isn't at the moment, but —'

'So how do you think it was done?'

'I'm not sure, although there is a prec —'

'Are there any similarities between these seven patients?'

'Not that I've noticed, yet, but —'

'I'm afraid I'm not convinced, Sister. What were you expecting me to do about it?'

'I'm sorry about that. I was hoping that we'd both go to the police.'

'There certainly isn't sufficient reason to do anything like that. Besides, we would have to go to the hospital manager first and I know that his reaction would be the same as mine.'

'Miss Whittington —'

'If there are any further deaths that worry you, come and tell me about them and I'll consider speaking to the hospital manager. Until then, we do nothing. Is that clear?'

'*Further* deaths? But I'm the one who has to —'

'Until then, we do nothing. *Is that clear*?' She didn't raise her voice. She didn't need to.

'Yes, Miss Whittington.'

'I'm quite sure you'll find that we now have a period with an unnaturally low death rate. It's the way things happen. Meanwhile, I suggest you attend to the other matter we discussed, and also write me a full report on how Mr Peters came to die unsupervised.'

As I walked angrily back down the corridor, I tried telling myself that she was a good nurse and a good administrator (both true) and that her reaction was only to be expected. It didn't help.

Back in the Duty Room, Mary told me that Mr Peters was now on life support for the purposes of transplant and that everything else was running smoothly. I decided not to talk to her about the 'other matter' until my temper had improved.

That night, I couldn't sleep for thinking about things. The next morning — Saturday — I left Mary in charge and went to the city's main police station.

Chapter 2

Other than to produce my driving documents once, I'd never been in a police station before — sheltered upbringing, I suppose. It was so unwelcoming.

Cream and brown paint and grubby tiles on which my shoes clacked.

A youth in a leather jacket and filthy jeans trendily torn at the knees sat on a chair with one foot balanced on the other leg, absently picking his nose. His eyes registered my arrival, otherwise he made no reaction. There was a counter with a glass hatch and a bell push with a notice: Please ring for attention. I rang.

After a few moments, a sergeant pulled back the sliding glass.

'Can I help you' — his eyes took in my uniform — 'ah, miss?' He was in his late thirties, plump, with a face that might once have been good-looking, but was now puffy and dissipated, with receding hair.

I lowered my voice. 'I'd like to speak to someone, in confidence, about a crime that may be — er — being committed.'

'A crime that may be being committed,' he repeated patronizingly. 'And what crime might that be, miss?'

'Murder,' I snapped. 'Can I speak to somebody, please?'

'Oh!' His eyebrows went up. 'I see. To whom would you like to speak, miss?' He had a flat Midlands accent.

'I don't know. Somebody in authority. And in confidence.'

'And you are . . .?'

I told him my name.

'If you'd like to take a seat, Miss Farewell' — he indicated to where trendy knees was sitting — 'I'll see if there's anybody available at the moment. Anybody in authority, that is.'

There were only three chairs and trendy knees was sitting in the middle one. I walked slowly over to the opposite wall and waited. Glanced at my watch. Shouldn't leave Mary on her own for too long.

I looked round. Trendy knees was staring at me, not looking away when our eyes met. I looked above his head, at a picture of a villainous-looking man and next to it, a young woman. I was too far away to read the writing, but I could hazard a guess as to what it said . . .

If someone doesn't come soon, I thought, I shall walk out of here. Glanced at my watch again. Five more minutes, I thought.

After three, a man in plain clothes looked round the door.

'Miss Farewell? Would you like to come through?' He held the door open and led me down a corridor. 'In here, please.'

It was a tiny room, just two chairs and a formica-topped table with a battered tin ashtray.

'Have a seat.' He indicated one of the chairs and we sat.

'I'm Detective-Inspector Anslow and I believe you want to talk about a possible murder.' He, too, had a Midlands accent, but not so pronounced — more pleasant.

'Inspector, I'm in a difficult position. I believe that a crime — murders — may have been committed in the hospital where I work. I went to my senior — my boss — about it. She wasn't very impressed and told me to do nothing. Told me not to contact the police. But I'm here and I'm asking for an assurance that our conversation is in complete confidence.'

He regarded me in silence for a moment. He had widely-spaced grey eyes, I noticed, and fair hair over a square, chunky, rather pleasant face.

'That could place us in a difficult position,' he said at last. 'If I were to agree with you that a crime —

murder — may have been committed, how could I remain silent?'

I glanced at the ashtray between us again, opened my bag and bought out my cigarettes.

'I hope you don't mind, Inspector. I don't usually smoke during the day, but that waiting room of yours got to me.'

He grinned. 'And its occupant, I daresay.' He pushed the ashtray towards me. When my cigarette was alight, he said, 'So what are we going to do, Miss Farewell?'

'If you were to go to my boss,' I said slowly, 'and tell her what I'd said, it would do me no good at all.'

'That wouldn't be the case if you were right, surely?' he said. Then, before I could answer, 'The best I can do for you is to give you my word that we won't speak to your superiors unless it becomes absolutely necessary. Will that do?'

I looked at his face. Could I trust him?

'I suppose it'll have to,' I said. Then, I told him my story. It sounded even less convincing in my ears than it had when I'd told Miss Whittington.

He listened without interrupting, other than to ask me to slow down once or twice while he took notes. When I'd finished, he looked at me pensively for a few moments, tapping his teeth with the end of his pen.

'Miss Farewell, is there anyone that you suspect might be doing this?'

I shook my head. 'No.'

'Someone on your ward perhaps who gives you a bad feeling, the creeps?'

'There's no one like that.'

'You've no ideas at all?'

'None, I'm afraid.'

'OK. D'you have any idea how the killings were carried out? What method was used?'

'No specific ideas, but there are precedents, as I'm sure you already know. There was the doctor last year who killed his patient with an injection of concentrated potassium chloride . . .'

'But that was a mercy killing, wasn't it?'

'Yes, but still an effective killing. And there was the case of the nurse in Thatchbury who killed four children with insulin, they weren't mercy killings. Nor the nurse in Germany who killed seventeen patients with the drug Catapresan, nor the nurses in Vienna who murdered forty-nine patients using a variety of drugs and physical means . . .'

'All right, all right, you've made your point.' He held up his hands in surrender. 'But wouldn't it be fairly obvious if a patient died immediately after they'd been given an injection?'

'If it was given intramuscularly, they wouldn't die immediately after. There would be a delay of two or three hours, maybe more.'

'Hmm. Handy for a killer.' He thought some more. 'Wouldn't these things be detected in a post-mortem?'

'Not unless you specifically looked for them. Even then, not always. And only a minority of patients who die in hospital are given a PM.'

'All right, but surely there's a limit to the number of people who can just come into a ward and give a patient an injection?'

'You'd be surprised how many, Inspector. There are thirty-five nurses on my ward, and half a dozen doctors. And patients on ITU are given a lot of drugs, often by injection. They are also frequently on a drip — something could be added to that.'

'But presumably you'd have records of all such treatments?'

'Yes, although there are an awful lot of them, and the fatal one probably wouldn't be recorded.'

He studied me for a few seconds. 'Miss Farewell, why don't you think your superior, the nursing officer, would believe you?'

I thought for a moment, then said, 'Because it sounds very improbable, I suppose. So it does, but as I said just now, there are precedents, aren't there?'

'Ye — es. Would you mind if I photocopied those case reports? And your statistical analysis. To show to *my* superiors.'

I hesitated. 'Very well. But please —'

'Not unless absolutely necessary,' he said, standing up. I handed him the reports and my analysis.

When he returned, he handed them back and said,

'That's as far as we can go for now. If I need to speak to you again, I'll ring your home number. Are you usually available in the evenings?'

'As often as not. Inspector, what will happen now?'

'Well, as I said, I'll have to take it to my superiors before I do anything else.'

'Then what?' I persisted.

'I can't be sure at this stage. In view of your request for confidentiality, it might be better if you didn't know.' He grinned to show it was a joke, then told me he'd contact me as soon as he heard something.

*

Mary was in the Duty Room when I got back. 'I thought you were only going to be half an hour,' she said reproachfully.

'I know, I'm sorry. Things took longer than I thought. Everything OK?'

'Nurse Armitage has gone off sick, although I suppose that's no great loss.' She lowered her voice. 'And Mr Peters has gone. They found matches for his kidneys in London.'

'I see.'

'Jo —' she looked at me curiously — 'd'you have a problem?'

'Problems, plural. And one of them concerns you, Mary.'

'Oh dear. Is that what the Witless wanted to see you about yesterday?'

'Yes. And it's *Miss Whittington* from now on.'

'Oh,' she began, 'that bad —'

'James is coming,' I said. 'We'll go into my office.'

'Dammit!' Mary said, after I'd finished, 'Nursing officers and matrons have had nicknames since time began, and not always flattering. You know as well as I do, Jo, that we have to have a . . . robust sense of humour here.' Her voice was controlled, but there were two angry red circles on her cheeks — she didn't like being rebuked.

'I know, Mary, and I agree — to an extent. But it was a bit dim of you to tell Nurse Hadley — loudly — not to leave the blood packs lying around because, and I quote: *It'll drive the Witless shitless*, when she was ten paces behind you.'

She smiled sheepishly. 'No, it wasn't too bright, was it?' She sighed. 'Would it help if I apologized to her — personally?'

'Best if you just looked . . . chastened for a while.'

'OK. I should be able to manage that. Sorry to have dropped you in it, Jo.'

'Not the best metaphor, in the circumstances,' I observed, and we both laughed.

Glad though I was to have that problem out of the way, it didn't help with the other, major, one. As I wrote up the report on Peters for Miss Whittington, my mind kept jumping about, wondering what the police were going to do.

Send someone incognito . . .? An image of the desk sergeant in nurse's uniform flashed in front of me — I smiled, then pushed it aside.

Or would they — someone senior to Anslow — decide to approach the hospital manager, despite my request?

They couldn't sack me for it, I thought, but it would do my prospects no good at all . . . and a small, desolate feeling formed in the pit of my stomach and grew. I was ambitious and when I'd been appointed senior sister in ITU at St Chad's after returning from Birmingham, I'd been really buoyed up, so sure that I was on my way. I couldn't bear to lose that feeling.

When the report had been typed, I debated for a moment whether to give it to Miss W personally or put it in the internal post. The latter, I decided. She'd be sure to say some-thing about THE PROBLEM, as I thought of it, and my face might give me away.

The rest of the day passed uneventfully and a little after five, I drove home to my terrace.

Although I'd lived there for nearly a year, walking up the path, opening the front door and hearing it close behind me with a solid snick still gave me a sense of pleasure. As a girl, I used to cycle round the city and I'd loved this street of Victorian artisans' cottages even then, although my parents, who owned a 'fifties semi, raised their hands in horror when I told them so. Still, that sort of attitude has changed now and my little terrace has become almost trendy.

I put on the kettle, kicked off my shoes and flopped on the sofa to open my letters — I have to leave before the postman comes.

The sleepless night had caught up with me and I felt almost too tired to get to my feet when the kettle boiled. That made me remember I had a loose arrangement to go out with Mary that evening — she would phone, she'd said earlier in the week. I was fairly sure she wouldn't now, not after I'd played the heavy with her this morning, and that suited me. Mary's company could be stimulating, and one or two of the parties we'd been to had been fun, but she could be very wearing. She was a divorcée who liked to 'play the field', which included toy boys. One evening when she'd set us up with a couple, I'd told her bluntly that as far as I was concerned, it was infra dig, and she'd called me a snob. She'd got the message though, and we'd remained friends — as I said, she could be great fun. But not tonight, Josephine, I said to myself.

I made some tea and thought about Inspector Anslow. There was something about him I liked, and I was glad now that I'd been to the police. The more I thought about it, the less worried I felt; it was as though I'd handed the whole problem over to them. Which only goes to show that police officers are every bit as good at giving false comfort as doctors.

Chapter 3

The next morning, I had a lie-in (till nine, anyway) then a leisurely breakfast over the Sunday paper before driving over to my parents' house for lunch.

They lived on the other side of Latchvale, in the same 'fifties semi I'd grown up in. They were very conservative, rather like Latchvale itself — an English cathedral city that had somehow found itself in the West Midlands. I was something of an afterthought: Mum was over forty when she had me, which meant she was nearer seventy than sixty now. Dad was even older.

They didn't repeat the experience (whether by design or default, I don't know) which meant that one way and another, I had rather an odd upbringing.

They sent me to the same small private school that Mum had been to (a survival even then) which believed in educating their 'gels' rather than gaining them qualifications. It gained me enough to become a nurse, though.

*

'Hello, Mum.'

'Hello, dear.'

We kissed cheeks.

'Would you like a cup of tea? Or a glass of sherry, perhaps?'

Yeeuch!

'I'd rather a coffee, if you wouldn't mind.'

'Very well, dear. Your father's in the lounge.'

I went through. He was dozing over the paper. I kissed his papery cheek.

'Hello, Dad.'

'Oh! Hello, Jo. I didn't hear you come in. How are you?'

'Fine, thanks. You?'

'I'm fine.'

Although I loved them both, we had nothing in common and it sometimes seemed to me as though the silences between us were more intimate than the conversations.

Lunch. Roast beef, potatoes and two veg . . .

'No more roast potatoes for me, thanks, Mum.'

'I can't think how you survive on what you eat, Jo.'

Table talk . . .

'Have you made any friends yet on your new ward?' She meant boyfriends.

'I'm a career girl, Mum. Too busy.'

'Such a shame when you stopped seeing Alan . . .'

Dr Alan Mitchell, with whom I went out for a year.

'That was ages ago, Mum. While I was still working in Birmingham.'

'Still, it *was* a shame. Do you ever hear from him now?'

'He got married last month.'

'Oh.' Pause. 'Well, I hope she's a nice girl. I liked Alan.'

So did I, I thought.

I loved my parents dearly, but I sometimes wondered by what accident of genetics they bred me.

*

I adored the autumn. The mornings were so fresh after the dusty overripeness of late summer, and the streets and half-timbered houses of the old part of the city seemed so clean. They'd been autumn-cleaned. I decided to walk through the park to work on Monday — it was only about a mile to the hospital. The sun highlighted the deep autumn green of the trees, and the pink sandstone of the city spires pricking above them. The air held a faint, earthy tang.

The first person I met in the main corridor was Mary.

'Sorry I didn't phone you on Saturday, but Hugo invited me to a bash at the university.'

'That's all right. I was shattered anyway. Did you have a good time?'

'Mmm, I did.' She paused. 'You're looking very healthy this morning.'

'I walked in.'

'That explains it. Well, here we are.' We turned into the lobby of the ward. 'Another day, another dollar.'

I followed her through, wondering why she'd used that rather dated expression. There was something rather dated about Mary generally: her name, and the way she'd bestowed a nickname on Miss W — no one called her Witless until Mary came. That got me wondering how old she was — she'd never told me. Late twenties? Early thirties? Older than me, anyway. And today she looked it, although the bone structure of her face could take it. Men found her slightly ravaged beauty attractive. But for how much longer, I wondered.

Bitch, Josephine . . .

Teresa Barlow, who'd been in charge of the graveyard shift, handed over to me and the day began.

First, check everything for the consultant's round at nine. The mundane: beds tidy, floors clean, equipment cleared away . . .

The detail: patients' notes, graphs, recordings all in order . . .

The technical: monitors functioning properly, life support systems, infusion drips . . .

Patients happy . . .

Our consultant, Mr Chorley, had a gift for making patients happy. He gave each one a portion of his undivided attention. His manner was so reassuring that even the most sick brightened up. And he didn't bully his house officers either; at least, not in front of the patients.

He was a small, slight man who always wore a dark suit and was consistently immaculate in appearance — unusual in a small man. He was balding, wrinkled, and his blue eyes were faded. He could so easily have been a figure of fun, but he wasn't.

'Good morning, Mr Ashbourne. How are you feeling today?'

'Fine, thank you, Doctor.'

'Fine — *all right*, or fine — *really fine*?'

A smile. 'Fine — all right.'

A quick look at the charts. 'Better than you were feeling yesterday, anyway?'

A vigorous nod.

'Chest pain?'

'Some. Here.' He indicated with his fingers.

'That's only to be expected at this stage. Let me look at this chart a moment. Hmm.' He showed it to the house officers. 'Any comments?'

'A good response to isosorbide. Steady progress.' Paul

Ridware, house officer: shiny black hair, dark complexion, smooth and sensual.

'Ye — es. What about this?' He pointed to a dip in the graph.

'Dosage a little too low?' Deborah Hillard, senior house officer: slim and assured, attractive, with curly auburn hair.

'What would you recommend?'

'Increase by five milligrams daily?'

'Yes. I'd agree with that.' He turned to Stephen. 'Can you organize that, please, Dr Wall?'

'Certainly, Mr Chorley.' He made a note.

Back to the patient. 'You're doing well, Mr Ashbourne. We'll be transferring you to the Coronary Care ward soon. Tomorrow, or perhaps the day after. We'll see.'

'Thank you, Doctor. I — er — thanks.'

'You're very welcome.'

Move on to next patient.

Including the beds in the isolation rooms, our ITU held only nine patients, so the ward round didn't take too long. And, pleasant man though Mr Chorley was, we all heaved a metaphorical sigh of relief when he'd moved on to the next ward.

Then, to work.

Organize changes in drug therapy. Take a patient off the monitors. Arrange for collection of blood samples.

Minor medication to relieve minor aches and pains, sore arms from infusions and venepunctures . . .

Mrs Peters rang, tearfully asking for Mr Peters's wedding ring which hadn't been with his other effects. I assured her it would be returned, thinking, *Oh my God, not a thief on top of everything else, please* . . .

Jenny Towers, the physiotherapist, arrived with a list of patients to see . . .

The ECG technician, Jacqui (with an i) Newborough, brought in her equipment, picked up her requests and started work . . .

Pat Drayton, phlebotomist (a fancy title for blood sample taker) picked up *her* requests and studied them for a moment.

'Susan not around?' James asked her.

'She's off for a fortnight,' replied Pat. 'Why? Aren't I good enough for you?' Put as a joke, but defensive all the same.

''Course you are, Pat. Beautiful, too. Just wondered, that's all.'

In fact, Susan King, our usual phlebotomist, was much better than Pat, who tended to be rather brutal when she couldn't find a vein first time.

'Pat . . .' Gail Colton, staff nurse, said. 'Try Mrs Weston's right arm today, would you? Her left's in a bit of a mess.'

'OK,' said Pat. 'But she's got terrible veins, that one. Really difficult to find.'

'All right, Pat. Just do your best. I'll be glad when Susan's back,' she continued in an undertone when Pat had gone, and we all agreed. Dumpy, unobtrusive Susan who quietly got on with the job; so gentle that several patients had said they literally couldn't feel a thing when she pushed her needle in . . .

'Jo,' said Gail, 'that deadbolt on the air-lock is sticking again . . .'

I went out with her to have a look.

'OK, I'll phone the engineer . . .'

Emma Riley approached me. 'Can I have a word please, Jo?'

'Sure. Let's go in here.'

We went into the empty rest room.

'Could I swap patients with James, please?' She was very red in the face, I noticed.

'What's the problem?'

'Mr Phillips, he's just too much. I know I'm a big girl now, but this morning, while I was adjusting his electrodes, he managed to feel my thigh with his right hand and stroke my breast with his left at the same time.'

She was really upset, I noticed.

'No problem. D'you want me to have a word with him?'

She shook her head. 'No, there's no point. He's not going to make it, is he?'

'No,' I agreed . . .

How strange, I thought. Emma, with her honey-coloured hair, honeypot face and body (I'd seen Stephen and Paul and James all drooling over her) so prim and proper — a churchgoer, I'd heard . . . and Mary, who looked so coolly beautiful, yet who could be truly wanton . . .

They were both good nurses, though — parts of the team I wouldn't have wanted to be without.

The door opened and James came in.

'Sorry, am I interrupting something?'

'No, we'd finished,' I said. 'In fact, it concerns you, James.'

'Oh?'

'Why don't you make us both a coffee while I tell you?'

'Sure.'

A wry smile touched his pale, pleasant face, with its slightly flattened features, as I explained why I wanted him to change patients with Emma.

'I'm not surprised,' he said. 'I saw him ogling you yesterday, Emma. Funny, isn't it,' he continued. 'How it's sometimes the most ill who are the randiest. As though they're making up for lost time.'

'Thank you, James,' I said, 'for that penetrating insight. Now how about that coffee?'

'Oh, right.'

I'd barely finished drinking mine when Miss Whittington's head appeared round the door.

'Sister Farewell, could I have a word, please?'

'Of course.' I put the cup down and went with her to my office.

'Your report on Mr Peters covered everything

satisfactorily. I don't think we need take the matter any further.'

'Oh, good. Thank you.'

'Have you spoken to Sister Tamworth?'

'Yes, I have. She accepts the criticism; in fact, she offered to apologize to you personally.'

'That won't be necessary.'

'That's what I told her.'

'Good.' She hesitated. 'And have you had time to reflect on the other matter?'

'Er — yes, I have.' Her look told me that more was required. 'I — er — I'll wait and see whether there are any more unexpected deaths, as you suggested.'

'Good. I'm quite sure you'll find that there won't be, and that things will even themselves out.' She paused. 'I notice you haven't taken any leave for some time. Perhaps you need a short break. Are many of your staff away at the moment?'

'Yes, several, including one of the sisters, Vivien Aldridge.'

'Ah, yes. When is she due back?'

'She's off for two weeks, so today fortnight.'

'Well, perhaps you could take some time off when she returns.'

'I'll bear that in mind,' I said.

'Good,' she said for a third time, and made for the door. 'Oh. Have you drawn the attention of your staff to Mr Chorley's talk tonight?'

Had I?

'I'll make sure I remind them, Miss Whittington.'

Damn! I thought as she left. I'd have to go myself and drag some of the others with me.

Mr Chorley gave a talk every two months on the care of cardiac patients — he had responsibility for the Coronary Care and Medical wards as well as ITU. He was an excellent speaker and it was to his credit that he gave of his time for the benefit of new staff, but when you'd heard it three times already, as I had, the prospect wasn't quite so alluring.

Chapter 4

I managed to bully half a dozen or so of the others into attending, and by seven was back at the hospital myself and on my way to the lecture theatre when I ran into Stephen.

'Still here, Jo?'

I explained about the talk and how I felt obliged to go myself, when so few of the others could.

'I'll come with you, then,' he said.

'Surely you've been to one of his talks before? Not that I mind you coming,' I added quickly.

We resumed walking.

'I did go to one when I first came here' — Stephen had only been at the hospital for a few months — 'but I was called out halfway through. Never seemed to have found the time since.'

We arrived and he held the door open for me.

The small lecture theatre was fairly well filled and we chose seats at the back — instinctively, perhaps. I could see Student Nurse Pete Hadley (Armitage was still off sick) nearer the front with two or three of the others.

The talk was opened by Dr John Cannock, St Chad's director of Pathology, who was chairman of the lecture group that year.

'It gives me very great pleasure,' he said in warm, rounded tones that issued from his large frame as though it were a sound box, 'to introduce my colleague, and friend, Richard Chorley . . .'

'That's rich, coming from him,' Stephen murmured. 'I'd have thought he'd have ducked out of this one.'

It was no secret that Mr Chorley and Dr Cannock had fallen out over the provision of laboratory testing in ITU and disliked each other intensely.

'He appreciates the irony, perhaps,' I whispered back.

Mr Chorley's talk itself lasted for about an hour, after which, Dr Cannock invited questions. It was while Paul Ridware was asking a particularly tedious one that Stephen touched my shoulder and breathed in my ear, 'Share a bottle with me in Luigi's?'

I smiled and nodded and we slipped out.

'My car's in the staff park,' I said when we were in the corridor.

'It's a nice evening,' he said. 'Why don't we walk?'

'Why not indeed?'

Although by now it was dark, a band of light lingered

in the west, and that, and the soft warm breeze made it good to be in the open air.

'I'm rather glad I went now,' I said, after we'd walked a little way. 'He . . .' I searched for the right words . . . 'He has a gift for making you feel useful, reasserting your faith in your job.'

'Perhaps he missed his vocation,' Stephen said lightly. 'Perhaps he should have been a cleric.'

'Oh, that would have been a waste.'

'Joking.' He held my arm as we crossed the road. 'So the Witless elicits in you the same fear she does in me,' he said when we reached the other side.

'How d'you mean?'

'The fact that you're here. That you came to the lecture.'

'It's more like healthy respect,' I said after a moment. 'Talking of which, I'd be grateful if you didn't refer to her by that name any more — not on the ward, anyway.'

He looked at me. 'I noticed Mary saying Miss Whittington in tones of reverence this afternoon,' he said. 'Was that your doing?'

I sighed. 'Yes.'

'Tell me.'

I told him.

'I'd prefer you kept it to yourself,' I said when I'd finished. 'For Mary's sake.'

'Of course.' He paused. 'And I hereby swear that the

words the Witless shall never be spoken by me again,' he added solemnly.

'Good.' I smiled to take any sting out of it.

Our footfalls echoed from the cobbles of pedestrianized street. The clock in the cathedral struck the half hour.

'It sounds rather like a clash of unsympathetic personalities,' he continued after a moment. 'Mary's and — uh — Miss Whittington's.'

'Yes,' I said, grinning at his tone.

'With you as piggy in the middle,' he said as we reached Luigi's and he held open the door for me.

'Thanks,' I said drily.

'Any preference?' he said as he went to the bar.

'Something white, if that's all right with you.'

'Chardonnay?'

'Fine.' I left him to it and found a table.

There weren't many customers, even for a weekday; the recession must have hit Luigi's pretty hard. It had been opened in the late 'eighties, which probably meant a big mortgage. It would be a shame if it closed, I thought, looking round. Dark wooden furniture, good quality too; stained floor, goodish pictures . . . Stephen arrived with the bottle and glasses.

'Cheers!' he said when he'd poured and we'd touched glasses. 'Mm, nice. What were we talking about . . .? Ah yes, Dick.'

'Dick?'

'Whittington. Had a cat and became Lord —'

'Ha, ha. And I don't think she'd appreciate the sobriquet Dick any more than the Witless.'

'Aha! You said it yourself!' He dropped his voice to a stage whisper. 'The Witless. I knew you'd say it eventually.'

'You're infantile,' I said, laughing nevertheless.

His eyes switched away for a moment. 'You have to be, in our job.'

'Our job . . .' I mused. 'Yes, I suppose you do.' I drank some more of the wine. It was delicious. 'Are you thinking of specializing in cardiology?'

He smiled, rather enigmatically. 'I'm not sure yet.'

'Where were you before you came to Latchvale?' I asked, curious.

'Birmingham.'

'You too? Which hospital?'

'Royal United.'

'So what brought you here? Latchvale's a bit of a back-water.'

'There was a vacancy here in Cardiology, so I took it, for the experience.'

Took it, I noticed, rather than applied for it.

'Did you train at the Royal?'

'No, London. But I moved to Birmingham for —'

'For the experience?' I finished for him. 'My, you have been around.'

He shrugged and smiled again. 'It's all useful in the end.'

'Where are you from, Stephen?'

'Stratford-on-Avon, originally. My father's still a GP there.'

'Nice spot. So what about you? Would you like to emulate Mr Chorley, or will you follow Father's footsteps?'

'That was pretty good, Jo. You obviously haven't had enough wine.'

He refilled my glass, then told me he hadn't made up his mind what he wanted to do yet, although his father wanted them to go into partnership together, so that they could raise the money to build their own private health centre.

'Is that really you?' I asked, a little surprised.

'I don't know. It does have its attractions.' He gave another enigmatic smile, and then switched the subject to why I'd taken up nursing. The evening was growing rosier as the level in the bottle dropped, but then he said something that reminded me that I'd been to the police just two days before to talk about murder, and I shivered suddenly.

'What's the matter, Jo? Someone just walk over your grave?'

'I think they might have done,' I replied, thinking aloud.

He sat up. 'Tell me.'

Can I trust you? I wondered, looking at his strong, English face. I wanted to, very much.

'You remember Mr Peters?' I began. 'Last Friday —
did it surprise you, him dying?'

'I suppose it did,' he said slowly. 'But patients do die
unexpectedly.'

'Yes, they do,' I agreed. 'But how many patients?'

That got his attention and I told him what I'd told
Miss W, although not about going to the police, since
it had directly contravened her orders.

'That's a hell of a thing, Jo,' he said at last. 'If it
wasn't for the fact it was you, and the statistics, I'd
think . . .'

'What would you think?' I demanded.

'That you were being . . . over-imaginative,' he said
quietly. Then: 'Look, I'm sorry. I know a bit about
statistics — why don't you show me?'

'Now?'

'Why not?'

'Well, the files are at my house, for one thing.'

He grinned. 'The devices we men'll adopt to gain
our wicked ends.'

'Oh, very droll. Can't you see I'm worried . . .?'

He covered my hand with his own. 'I'm sorry, Jo. I
was . . . trying to help, I suppose. Do let me have a
look. Your house isn't far from here, is it?'

*

'I'm not sure you should have used probability limits
in this instance,' he said, frowning over my calculations

some thirty minutes later. 'How much d'you actually know about statistics?'

'Not much, beyond probability limits.'

'For another thing, you've used percentages here, of the numbers of patients, where you should have used the numbers themselves.'

'But I thought percentages would be more —'

'And the test you should really have applied is the chi-square test, possibly with Yates' correction. Look — have you got a pencil and paper?'

I found them and he showed me how, if I'd used a different method, the number of deaths wouldn't have been significant.

'I've never really understood statistics,' I said with a sigh.

'Statistics can be made to prove — or disprove — anything,' he said gently. 'You must have heard the old saying: *There are lies, damned lies, and statistics.*'

I smiled. 'Yes. But I'm still worried, Stephen. I still *feel* that there have been too many deaths, and of the wrong patients.'

'Woman's intuition?' He covered my hand again.

'Yes, damn you!' I said, snatching it away.

'Jo . . .' he took it again, held it. 'I'm sorry. Listen — I'll look into every one of these cases you've got listed here, and after that we'll both keep an eye on things, and if it happens again — oh, in the next week or so — we'll do something about it. A deal?'

'All right,' I said. 'A deal. Thanks, Stephen.'

'This has really been getting to you, hasn't it, Jo?'

'Yes.'

'You poor old thing.'

There was a moment of absolute stillness, then he leaned over and gently kissed me.

Chapter 5

There is no feeling in the world to match the high you get at the beginning of a new affair. Everything around you is sharpened, three-dimensional, more real.

Stephen had left sometime during the night and although I hadn't slept for a while afterwards, now, as I walked through the park to the hospital, I felt glorious. The autumn colours pulsed, the sky shimmered with blue, bringing alive the pink sandstone of the cathedral's three spires — the Ladies of the Vale . . . and as I looked at them, I suddenly understood why they'd been named that.

It had always seemed odd to me that a spire, that most phallic of symbols, should be called a lady, but that morning, as their delicate shapes hung as though suspended above the trees in the autumn air, I felt I'd never seen anything so graceful, elegant, so feminine.

And *savant*, I thought. They must be, after watching over six centuries of sinning humanity.

'Have you been at the drugs cabinet again?' Mary demanded after I'd arrived. 'Something's certainly got into you.'

'Clean, healthy living,' I replied. 'You should try it some time.'

'Ugh! No thank you.'

Stephen behaved to me as he always had, other than to give me a fleeting wink during the ward round when no one was looking. We lunched together and arranged to meet in the evening.

He was as good as his word, and over the next few days, looked into all seven of the cases on my list, going through them with me afterwards. As he said, each taken on its own was not suspicious, and without the statistical evidence, the number wasn't significant; just a run of bad luck.

On Friday morning, I phoned Inspector Anslow to apologize and withdraw my statement.

'You're sure about that?' he asked me.

'Yes, I am. I do hope you hadn't actually started taking any action . . .'

'Not really. I passed it upstairs, as I told you I would, and haven't heard anything since. I'll tell them it was a false alarm.'

'I'm terribly sorry, Inspector . . .'

'That's all right, Miss Farewell. Better this way

than you'd kept silent when there really was something.'

I thanked him and rang off.

Later that day, when I declined to go to a party with her, Mary said, 'It's Stephen, isn't it?'

'How did you know?'

'The way you've been looking at him. Proprietorial. Don't get too fond of him, because it won't last.'

'Whatever makes you say that?'

'Stephen never allows himself to become committed.'

'How d'you know? With respect, Mary, I have known him longer than you.'

She hesitated, then said, 'You haven't, actually. I worked with him at the Royal United.'

'I see.' And was that all you did, I wondered, but didn't say anything.

'He's self-centred,' she continued. 'Ruthless. He picks up women and discards them like . . . like playing cards. All lovey-dovey one minute, then . . .' She made a chopping motion with her hand. 'The only thing he's committed to is his career.'

'What makes you think I want it to last?' I said lightly.

'Because I know *you*.'

You're just jealous, I told myself, and tried to forget it.

*

Friday and Saturday nights, he stayed at my house, and on Sunday morning, I made him breakfast in bed before going round to my parents. I felt duty bound to go, especially since we had other plans for the following weekend. Anyway, he grabbed me and said, 'I think I'd rather have you for breakfast.'

'I can't, Stephen! I told Mum I'd be round . . .'

But I did.

*

The next week passed by uneventfully. Armitage came back, looking better for her enforced rest. (Her doctor had written *nervous exhaustion* on her sick-note, and perhaps he was right.)

I saw Stephen most evenings, and on Friday, we went to stay for a couple of nights in Montgomery, a time-warp of a town on the Welsh Marches. I loved every minute, although I couldn't help noticing Stephen had become slightly restive by Sunday. We had to come back fairly early because he was on standby. We bought a Chinese takeaway which we had in his flat in the doctors' block where he still lived.

I knew that he didn't like smoking and had reduced my consumption accordingly, but for some reason, I felt desperate for a cigarette afterwards and asked him for an ash-tray.

His irritation was palpable.

'It's beyond me, Jo,' he said, 'that someone of your intelligence, who knows all the risks, should still smoke.'

'I don't smoke very much,' I said defensively. 'Hardly

at all during the day, and perhaps ten or so in the evening. Less, when I'm with you.'

'In that case, it shouldn't be too difficult for you to give it up altogether. Seriously, Jo, there's a good clinic here at the hospital, and —'

'Please don't try and change me, Stephen. When I want to give it up, I will. But in my own time.'

He shrugged and changed the subject, and shortly afterwards, his phone went and he was called away.

'I'll see you during the week,' he said. 'Not sure exactly when, since I'm on standby for most of it. I'll be in touch.'

He kissed me gently enough before he left, but there was something missing.

Or am I imagining it, I wondered to myself later in the darkness of my bedroom as I tried to sleep. I hoped so, because I was becoming fond of him and was already regretting my outspoken independence. Mary's words came back to me.

*

Monday morning. Foul weather and the beginning of an even fouler week. Mary was on night duty, but Viv Aldridge was back, as was Susan King. Viv very tanned after a fortnight in the Bahamas with her boyfriend; Susan as pale as ever after two weeks on some retreat in the north with the religious sect she belonged to.

'Did you have a good time?' I asked her.

Her large, rather flat face, with its frame of pale, gingery hair, lit up. 'Yes, I did, thank you, Sister. I'm glad to be back, though.'

'We're glad to have you back,' I said.

'And so say all of us,' said Sophie Marsh, staff nurse. 'Not to mention the poor bloody patients.'

Susan said nothing, but looked quietly pleased.

Viv said, 'It may be of passing interest to hear that I had a good time as well.'

James snorted. 'Just one look at you is enough to tell us that. You must have put on a stone at least.'

'Why, thank you, kind sir.' She did a very creditable mock curtsey. Her christian name suited her; she was both vivid and vital, overflowing with life and sexuality. 'And aren't you glad *I'm* back?'

'Ye — es,' James said. 'You don't have such a tangible effect on the patients as Susan, though. You should've seen some of their arms after Pat had finished —'

'Thank you, James,' I interrupted. 'There are some things better left unsaid. And aren't you supposed to be looking after Mr Phillips?'

'Yes'm.' He sketched a salute. 'To hear is to obey,' he intoned, and was gone before I could think of a suitably crushing reply. The week was shaping up nicely already, and Mrs Sutton arrived half an hour later.

She'd taken an overdose of amitriptyline — an anti-depressant drug — a couple of hours or so beforehand and had been found comatose. Although her stomach had been pumped out, the drug can have serious after-effects on the heart, which is why she was in ITU.

O/Ds always irritate me (although I do my best not to show it), whether suicide was genuinely intended or not. They unnecessarily absorb resources that could be put to better use elsewhere. (And I suspect that when they don't die, they didn't really intend it. People who truly want to kill themselves usually make sure they take enough to do the trick, and leave enough time for it to work.)

She was about thirty; a fluffy blonde creature whose very softness told you she'd been pampered. I said as much to Viv after we'd seen her.

'Don't you realize who she is?' Viv said to me in an undertone.

'Should I?'

'She's Len Sutton's wife.'

'Well, I'd assumed she must have been married to a Mr Sutton of some species, although I hadn't realized it was a Len . . .'

'You mean you don't know who Len Sutton is?'

'No, I don't.'

'You have led a sheltered life, Jo. Len Sutton has a finger in every scam in the West Midlands.'

'Oh, a racketeer. I don't have your informed back-ground, Viv.' Her boyfriend's a solicitor.

'Still, I'd have thought you would have heard of him. The filth have been after him for years, without conspicuous success as yet.'

'Well, I hadn't.' I paused. 'I imagine she'll be transferred to a private hospital before too much longer.'

'She'll be here for a few days yet — it was a pretty big dose she took.'

'You think she meant it, then?'

'I do, yes.' It was her turn to pause. 'I wonder why? You wouldn't have thought she'd have wanted for anything, would you?'

'Except love, perhaps.'

Viv looked at me. 'You're rather a softy underneath it all, aren't you, Jo?'

But Mrs Sutton didn't seem to be short of even that when I saw her with her husband the next day.

He'd come in hesitantly, which surprised me when I realized who he was, holding a large bunch of flowers. He asked for Mrs Sutton in a Birmingham accent you could have stood a spoon in.

I told him, then said, 'I'm very sorry, but we don't allow flowers to be left by the bedside.'

'Oh? Why's that, then?'

'They might spread infection. I'll show you a place you can put them where she can see them.'

He grunted, but didn't demur.

He was a short, compact man; shorter than her, I guessed, and at least twenty years older. He had a broad face with beady brown eyes, small ears and nose, a hard mouth and less hair on the top of his head than on the backs of his hands. He wore well-cut slacks and a rather sharp blazer.

'She'll be all right, will she, Sister?' he asked anxiously after he'd left the flowers, and I assured him she would.

When I went through the ward twenty minutes later, he was holding her hands while she looked adoringly back at him.

I caught the words: 'Oh, Len, why didn't you say?' as I passed.

He came into the Duty Room before he left.

'Thank you, Sister,' he said almost humbly. 'You'll look after her, won't you?'

'Of course we will, Mr Sutton.'

How strange, I thought, when he'd gone. The last type of people you'd have thought would be a devoted couple. But that's what they were.

The phone rang. It was Mary, although I didn't recognize her at first.

'Jo, I'm terribly sorry, but I've got the most God-awful dose of flu. I just wouldn't get through tonight.'

'All right, Mary,' I said slowly. 'Have you any idea when you'll be back?'

'Not really. I'm sorry, Jo.'

'OK, Mary. Let us know how you are tomorrow.'

Damn, I thought as I put the phone down. We were already a staff nurse short on that shift. And Clare

Burton, the 'spare' sister for that week, was on leave for two days. I couldn't really ask Viv . . .

I'd have to do it myself. Damn, damn, *damn*!

I cleared as much paperwork as I could and went home just after two, hoping to get some sleep.

Some hope! I never find it easy sleeping before night duty at the best of times; my biological clock doesn't like it, but that afternoon, it was impossible. I was too keyed up, partly because I was thinking about Stephen, partly because, for some reason, I was filled with a vague apprehension.

I don't believe in omens or anything similar, but that night, while I was on duty, Mrs Sutton died.

Chapter 6

There was no warning.

Teresa handed over to me at midnight, reporting no particular problems. It happened twenty-five minutes after that.

I was at the nurses' station looking over some reports when the alarm went, and I hurried over to Mrs Sutton's bed. Gail already had her night clothes off and was giving her external heart massage.

'Ventricular fibrillation,' she said as I arrived. I glanced up at the monitor to confirm it, then quickly drew the screens around the bed.

Deborah Hillard and the rest of the crash team arrived less than a minute later. She looked at the monitor, then at Gail. 'When did it happen?'

'Two minutes ago. Less.'

'OK.' She looked at Mrs Sutton's face as it lay to one

side; the mouth slack. 'Intubate and oxygen, please, Graham,' she said to the anaesthetist. 'A hundred mil of sodium bicarb, intravenous,' to Jane Bromley, staff nurse. As she spoke, she checked that the defibrillator paddles were well smeared with electrode jelly before handing one to Nicky Twycross, the other staff nurse.

'Ready?'

Gail had stepped back. Jane completed the injection. Deborah and Nicky placed their electrodes either side of the heart and Deborah administered the shock. Mrs Sutton jerked, as did the trace on the recorder before settling back into the fibrillation pattern.

But, as with Peters, I knew it wasn't going to work and a dizzying sickness grew and spread from the pit of my stomach.

They went on trying for three-quarters of an hour, then brain stem death tests were carried out and she was pronounced dead. Deborah, hollow-eyed with fatigue, rang Mr Sutton herself. He arrived twenty minutes later.

If I hadn't been so busy organizing Last Offices (washing and laying out the body) and so wrapped in my own misery, it might have occurred to me to warn Deborah. It was only when I heard the familiar accent shouting: *'You mus' be out of your tiny fucken mind,'* that I realized she must have asked for permission for organ transplant.

Then there was a noise as he pushed his way into

the air-lock, Deborah saying: 'You'll disturb the other patients,' and Sutton replying: 'I don't give a fuck about the other patients, I want *her*!' He was pointing at me.

I hurried forwards to try and prevent him leaving the air-lock.

'Mr Sutton, I'm truly sorry —'

'Don't give me that, you bitch. You said you'd take care of her. This what you call taking care? Eh?'

Deborah hurried out.

'Please believe me,' I tried again. 'We did everything possible —'

He lashed out, the back of his hand caught my mouth and I staggered against the door . . .

'Someone's gonna pay for this, lady, an' I'm lookin' at *you* . . .'

He hit me again and something inside snapped.

'Why don't you find the one who really killed her,' I shouted, 'and take it out on —' I broke off as he stared at me.

'Wha'd'ya mean?'

'Nothing. I — I didn't mean anything —'

He caught my wrist, bent it, dragging me towards him . . .

'Yes, you did' — his face closed in, unshaven, his breath sour — 'I can see you did. Wha'd'ya mean, *the one who really killed her*?'

'*You*!' I said desperately. 'I meant you, for making her so unhappy that she —'

The door behind opened and Gail's voice snapped, 'Let her go!'

'You keep outa this!' His eyes flicked over to her, although he kept hold of my wrist.

'Let her go, or I'll —'

Then two security guards burst in and grabbed him — he released me and tried to hit one of them . . . Fortunately, the other spoilt his aim . . . Then, realizing he couldn't win, he relaxed and allowed himself to be led away. He turned and gave me a look just before the air-lock door swung shut behind him.

An arm went round my shoulder — Gail. Deborah ran over to me.

'Are you all right, Jo? You're bleeding, let me have a look . . .'

''S nothing,' I mumbled. 'Cut lip.'

'I'm so sorry I left you with him . . . I didn't think for a moment he'd . . .'

''S all right. You did the right thing . . .'

She took over from Gail, saying to her, 'Coffee, with plenty of sugar. I'll take her to the rest room.'

She led me through, sat me down. I found my bag, took out a cigarette and guided it to my lips. 'Sorry, Debbie, but I must.'

She gave the ghost of a smile. 'Well, under the circumstances, I suppose . . . let me have a look at your lip first.'

She gently pulled it up. 'Hmm. Fairly superficial. Try

washing your mouth with Listerine.' She put a hand under my chin. 'Move your jaw around . . . does that hurt?'

'No,' I mumbled.

'Good — nothing broken, then.'

Gail came in with the coffee. 'I put plenty of milk in so you could drink it straight away,' she said.

I took a mouthful and lit the cigarette. 'Is everything all right in there?'

'Don't worry about it. A couple of patients woke up, that's all. Nicky and Jane are calming them down. I'll go and check them now.'

'D'you want me to call the police?' Deborah asked as Gail left.

'No,' I said. 'There's no point. I'd only make a very bad enemy.'

She looked at me curiously. 'How d'you mean? I'd have said you already had one.'

I told her what Viv had told me about Len Sutton.

'It's my own fault,' I said as I finished. 'It should have occurred to me he'd do something like that. I didn't take her seriously enough.'

'It sounds to me as though we should get the police,' Deborah said.

'I'll think about it. Please — can we leave it at that for the moment?'

'All right,' she said doubtfully. 'If you're sure that's what you want . . .'

I had another coffee, another smoke, then washed my mouth with Listerine and felt almost back to normal. Except for the fact that Mrs Sutton made the eighth.

*

That thought nagged away at me all through the long hours of the shift, and as soon as I'd handed over to Viv at eight, I rang Stephen at his flat.

'It's Jo. I've got to speak to you. I'm coming over now.'

'Can it wait till I get in? I'm on duty in half an hour.'

'No. Honestly, Stephen, I must see you now.'

'Ahh . . . all right.'

About five minutes later, he opened the door and his eyes widened as he saw me.

'My God, Jo! What's happened?' My lip had ballooned after the attack and I had a livid bruise over one cheek-bone.

'Let me come in and I'll tell you.'

He sat me down on his sofa and took the armchair opposite. I gave him all the facts, excepting what I'd let slip to Sutton.

'How absolutely appalling,' he said when I finished. 'I think you were probably right to be cautious about involving the police, though,' he continued slowly, 'if Sutton's as dangerous as you say.'

'Stephen, the reason I was cautious is that I think Mrs Sutton was murdered. Like the others.'

His eyes opened wide for a moment, then closed as he said tiredly, 'Oh, my God, I thought we'd sorted all that out. All right. You'd better tell me.'

My tongue touched my lips — lip, rather.

'She was getting better. She was over the worst. It was what . . . thirty-six? Forty hours since she'd taken the amitriptyline. She was young, healthy. There's just no earthly reason why she should have had a heart attack then. We must get a post-mortem on this one, Stephen . . .'

'But you know as well as I do, Jo, that amitriptyline O/Ds can still be at risk of cardiac effects up to six days later . . . D'you know how much she took?'

'Er . . . 1500 milligrams, I think.'

'A hell of a lot, then. She could still . . .'

'But Stephen, a post-mortem would show us once and for all . . .'

He let out a breath. 'OK, OK. I'll speak to Debbie, see what she thinks —'

'You're not going to tell her about —?'

'I'll only ask her about the medical aspects — OK? Now you get home and try to get some rest.'

'But Stephen . . .'

'Look, Jo, I'm on duty in ten minutes and I daren't be late. Go home and I'll either come round or ring you later today. I promise. OK?'

He squeezed my hand before gently pulling me to my feet and seeing me out.

I suppose he couldn't really have done any more, I thought as I drove slowly back.

He could have put you to bed at his place . . . a small voice answered.

I was trembling with exhaustion when I got home, and pausing just to brush my teeth and rub some cream into my bruised face, went straight to bed.

But not to sleep — every nerve in my body seemed to be jangling and jostling at once . . .

I got up, made some tea and had a cigarette. Then, after some hesitation, I poured myself a strong whisky. As its warmth spread from my stomach to the rest of my body, I began to relax.

I glanced at my watch. Josephine Farewell, I thought, drinking whisky at ten in the morning. Whatever next?

But it did make me feel better and as I settled back into bed, the worst of the trembling and jangling seemed to have gone, and after a while, I slipped into an uneasy sleep.

About four or five hours later, I surfaced with great difficulty, reaching for the phone before I realized it was the doorbell. Stephen!

'All right, all right, I'm coming!' I shouted as I ran down the stairs, tying the sash of my dressing gown.

If I hadn't been so muzzy, maybe I'd have checked who it was, but it probably wouldn't have made any difference . . .

Anyway, as soon as I slipped the chain, the door was thrown in my face and two creatures: one black, one white, not long evolved from apes, pushed their way in. Len Sutton strolled in after them.

Chapter 7

As the white ape shut the door, I said, 'If you touch me, I'll scream.'

Sutton looked at the black ape, who put his hand in his pocket and brought something out. There was a snick and a blade sprang from his hand. It flashed in the light from the window.

'You won't scream, Sister,' Sutton said flatly.

My eyes were hypnotized by the blade. Sutton said, 'All I want from you is answers. What did you mean last night about I should go after the one that really killed Sharon?'

'I didn't mean anything. I was overwrought. It was a mistake.'

He nodded to the black ape with the knife, who took a quick step forwards . . . the blade became a glinting arc and the sleeve of my dressing gown fell loose, slashed halfway up the arm. I had neither heard nor felt anything. My skin was untouched.

'What did you mean?'

My back pressed into the wall and I realized I'd been walking backwards. 'I — I suppose I meant you. Because . . .'

'No you didn't, Sister. You meant somethin' else. What was it?' He didn't raise his voice and his very calmness was as frightening as the knife.

'I don't *know.*' I heard my own voice rise to a squeak. 'I swear I —'

But he'd nodded again, and once more the blade flickered . . . and the sash fell softly round my feet as the dressing gown gaped open.

'I'll ask you once more. What did you mean?'

They were all staring at me. The black knifeape was staring at the material of my nightdress over my breasts, but there was nothing lascivious in his gaze, only professionalism.

My tongue touched my lip. 'All right. Please, can I sit down?'

'No. Jus' talk.'

'All right.' I swallowed. 'It has seemed to me, over the last two months, that . . . more people have died in that ward than should have died. It seemed to me that your wife may have been another.'

'It seemed to you . . . is that all?'

'I did a statistical analysis. Statistically, the deaths shouldn't have happened.'

His eyes stared back at me.

'Have you told anyone?'

'My nursing officer.'

'What did she say?'

'She didn't believe me.'

'D'you tell anyone else? The police?'

'Yes. A detective-inspector, but —'

'What did he say?'

'He said he'd pass it to his superiors, but . . .'

'How long ago?'

'I — about two weeks.'

'Two weeks? They done anything?'

'No. I was trying to tell you, I told him later it was a false alarm.'

'Why? Why d'you do that?'

'Because I also told my . . . my boyfriend — a doctor — and he persuaded me I was wrong.'

He stared at me. 'So now you're sayin' you were wrong after all?'

'*No*! No. I was never really convinced, and your wife's death made me realize I was right . . .' It occurred to me, too late, that I should have let him think I *had* been wrong — neurotic, in fact.

'How long was this after you first told them? The police?'

'A few days — a week.'

'D'you tell anyone else?'

I shook my head. 'No.'

He thought for a moment, still staring at my face.

'How many of these . . . killings?'

'Your wife was the eighth I thought was sus —'

'*Eighth*? Eight killings and no one does a fuck about it? What kinda fucken hospital is this?'

'I didn't suspect anything myself' — I gabbled — 'until the fifth or sixth . . . each one seemed like an ordinary death until you took them all together.'

His mouth was still working. 'Sounds more like *in-fucken*-competence to me . . .'

His outline became fuzzy, his voice indistinct . . .

'If I don't sit down, I'm going to faint.'

'Aw right, aw right.' He waved me to the sofa. I sank on to it and closed my eyes.

He was talking to his apes . . .

'Sounds like some kinda sicko, like the one in Thatchbury . . .'

'Maybe it's just in her mind, boss . . .'

'Naw. I don't think so . . .'

'Me neither . . .'

'Think the filth're doin' anythin' about it?'

'Naw. Not if she told them not to.'

'But they might. Y' can never tell with the filth. Why not make her ring an' ask?'

''Cos it might get them sniffin' round again, that's why not.'

I felt his shadow loom over me.

'Listen, Sister. You told the police to forget it and you heard nothin' since, right?'

'Yes.'

He looked at the others. 'Typical filth. Can't recognize real villains. Right. Listen, Sister, I want the names of the people you think were rubbed out; when they died, everythin'. An' your stastistycall whatsit. Got that? An' then I want the names of all the staff an' what hours they work. An' I want you to think *hard* about who did it — right?'

'I tell you, I've no idea,' I said tiredly.

'Well, you'd better get some ideas, fast. Either someone killed her, like you said, or, like I said, it was incompetence. *Your* incompetence.' He paused to let this sink in, then said, 'How long will it take you? To get the names together?'

'A day. Two days.'

'You got a day. What time d'you get back here in the morning?'

'It depends. About nine.'

'Polo' — he indicated the black knifeape — 'will collect it tomorrow morning at nine-thirty. An' when I've seen it, I'll be asking you some more questions. An', Sister, one more thing. Look at me . . .'

Unwillingly, I raised my eyes to his . . .

'*Don't* go to the filth about me — right? For two reasons. First' — he touched a finger — 'it'll be the word of the three of us against you. An' secondly, 'cos Polo here won't like it.'

Polo flourished the knife and grinned down at me.

Sutton turned and walked to the door. The white ape scurried over to open it for him.

'An', Sister . . .' he said tiredly, looking round at me, 'get some clothes on.' Then the door closed and they were gone.

I sat, frozen.

Time passed.

I stood, robot-like, and made for the stairs. Get some clothes on, he'd said. To hear is to obey.

I found some jeans and a sweater and stumbled back downstairs. Stared at the whisky bottle awhile, then slowly rose from the sofa and poured myself one. Then another. Found my cigarettes.

Stephen . . . he'd still be on duty, but I had to speak to him.

I lifted the receiver, dialled. Had him paged.

'Dr Wall speaking.'

'Stephen, it's Jo . . .'

'Jo! I said I was going to phone you — you needn't have bleeped me.'

'Stephen —'

'Listen' — he lowered his voice — 'you've no need to worry any more about Mrs Sutton. I've spoken to Debbie and she says there was absolutely nothing untoward about her death. Tragic, but nothing sinister . . .'

'Stephen —'

'She also told me what a shock you had last night.

It was probably that that gave you the idea. We'll talk about it later.'

'But, Stephen, he was here, at my house.'

'Who was?'

'Sutton, with two thugs. He threatened me.'

Pause. 'Why?'

'Well . . . I let something slip last night. I was shocked, as you said, and . . .'

'Let something slip about what?' he demanded.

I swallowed. 'The murders.'

Tiredly: 'Oh, my God! Jo, there haven't *been* any murders.' Pause. 'Listen to me carefully. I think you will have to go to the police now, but the only chance you've got for them to take you seriously is to admit from the outset that you made a mistake.' *You* go to the police, not *we*, I noticed through my misery. 'Have you got that, Jo? Then, maybe they'll be able to get Sutton off your back.'

'But I can't go to the police, Stephen. Sutton'll deny it and it's three to one . . .'

I heard him talking to someone at the other end, then: 'I'm sorry, Jo, I've got to go now. I'll be in touch. Go to the police and tell them you made a mistake.'

I sat, frozen.

Time passed.

What could I do?

I lit another cigarette.

Go to my parents?

But what could they do? They wouldn't understand. It wouldn't be fair on them. And Sutton would simply find me and threaten them, too . . .

Stephen was right, it had to be the police, or at any rate, Anslow. I found the number of the station and keyed it in.

'Latchvale Police, can I help you?' It was the fat slob behind the desk.

'Inspector Anslow, please.'

'He's not on duty at the moment, I'm afraid.'

'When will he be? On duty.'

'Not until Monday, I'm afraid. He's away on leave tomorrow.'

I closed my eyes.

'Perhaps I can help you. It is Miss Farewell, isn't it?'

'That's right. Could you possibly give me his home number, please? This is rather important.'

'I'm sorry, but we're not allowed to do that,' he said, not sorry at all. 'Perhaps if you were to tell me what the problem is . . .'

'No, thank you.' I banged the receiver back and fumbled for another cigarette.

Time passed.

Mary . . . but she was ill.

I rang her anyway, but knew somehow after the first ring that she wasn't going to answer it.

Too ill? Or otherwise occupied with one of her toy

boys . . . Irresponsible Mary — could I really have confided in her?

Yes! Yes . . . the receiver slipped from my fingers into its cradle.

Time passed.

Who could I talk to?

I tried a cousin in Birmingham I was close to once, but her husband, whom I didn't like much, told me she wouldn't be back until late . . .

All my friends had moved away, in spirit as well as place . . . but that hadn't really mattered while I had my career . . .

Without warning, I burst into tears. I could feel them coursing down my face, stinging my cheeks; I could feel my body convulsing with the sobs until it felt as though I had stomach cramps . . .

That was the curious thing. I couldn't stop crying, and yet another part of me seemed to be looking on, measuring, thinking: *So this is what despair is really like* . . .

It can't be happening, not to me . . . but it is . . .

After a while, I stopped crying, but through exhaustion, not because it had made me feel any better.

I looked at my watch, it was nearly seven — only five hours before I was on duty again. I felt so exhausted I thought I might sleep, but when I tried, everything just went round and round in my head . . .

I got up and made some more tea, then had a bath,

hoping it would relax me. It seemed to, but the moment I was in bed again, everything came back . . .

The alarm went — I must have dozed off after all. I felt awful — unrefreshed, dull headache — and it occurred to me to ring in sick, like Mary . . .

But what good would it do? Besides, I had to collect the information for Sutton — oh, yes — there was no way I could avoid doing that now . . .

I pulled on my uniform and dragged myself to the hospital.

I could never do justice to the next eight hours. I made mistakes, a lot of mistakes. Walked into things, knocked things over. A couple of times I felt so dizzy, I had to go and sit down.

Deborah asked me if I was all right.

'Just tired,' I said. 'I couldn't sleep.'

'After last night, I'm not really surprised.'

She sounded sympathetic, and for a moment, I was tempted to confide in her to relieve my heavy heart, but then she continued in a sharper tone, 'Stephen tells me you were unhappy about Mrs Sutton's death?'

'Well, yes, I was a bit. Didn't you think —?'

'We did all we could, you know.' She was defensive, hostile almost — what had Stephen been saying to her? 'There was nothing anybody could do about it. It was nobody's fault.'

'No,' I said dully.

I was too exhausted to give much thought to getting

the information together for Sutton, although I realized I'd have to find something for him. There were the notes about the dead patients I'd originally made and shown to Miss Whittington, together with the statistical analysis — they were both still at home.

I couldn't face trying to sort through all the recent work rotas, so at the end of the shift, I simply photo-copied the list of all the staff in ITU and their grades. After that, I dragged myself home.

When I got to my door, I couldn't find my keys. They weren't in my bag, nor in the car. I must have left them at work.

There's no back way into the terraces as such, a factory building forms the wall at the end of the garden, but there's a gate from my neighbour's. I knocked at their door and they let me through. I kept a spare key to the back door in my shed.

Once inside, I felt dizzy and just wanted to lie down. When was it Polo was coming? Nine-thirty, wasn't it? I made a coffee and sat on the sofa to wait.

Doorbell ringing . . . I'd dozed off. I picked up the envelope with the information and took it to the door, so that he wouldn't have an excuse to come in. Opened it on to the chain.

Not Polo.

A smaller man — white, rather hard looking.

'Sister Farewell?'

Another of Sutton's men . . .?

'Yes?'

'My name's Jones, I'm from the Department of Health. You made a rather disturbing allegation to the police a couple of weeks ago and I wondered if we might talk about it . . .'

Chapter 8

'You'd better come in.' I undid the chain. I hadn't really taken in what he'd said.

He came in almost hesitantly, holding something out. 'Don't you want to see my identification?'

'If you like.' I shut the door, then gazed at the plastic card he was holding.

I felt him staring at me. 'Are you all right?' he asked.

'Of course I'm all right,' I shouted back at him. 'People are being murdered in my ward and no one'll believe it except a Birmingham gangster who's threatened to knife me unless I . . . I thought you were him.'

'Unless what?' he said quickly.

'Unless I give him this' — I held up the envelope — 'information about the patients who've died, and the staff on the ward . . . he thinks he can find out who . . .'

'And you're expecting him now?'

'His sidekick, Polo . . . I thought you were him.'

'What time's he coming?'

'Nine-thirty, he said.'

He looked at his watch. 'Twenty-past . . . stay here a moment, would you?' He made for the door.

'Where are you going?' I cried.

'Just to my car to get something.'

I waited in the open doorway — couldn't bear the thought of him driving away . . . A car door slammed and he reappeared.

'Tell me how this gangster got involved,' he said, when he was back inside. 'What's his name?'

'Sutton. Leonard Sutton.' I tried to gather my wits. 'His wife, she died in my ward, he attacked me and I told him she'd been murdered. Then he came round here with a couple of thugs . . .'

'Here, to this house?'

'Yes . . .'

'When was this?'

'Yesterday. He threatened me; ordered me to get him the information about the patients and staff; told me one of his thugs — Polo — would come here this morning and collect it.'

'Is that it?' He pointed to the envelope. 'The information?'

'Yes.'

'Let me have it. D'you have a phone?'

77

I gave him the envelope and showed him the phone. 'Go over to the window and watch for him while I —'

'He might see me.'

'So what if he does? You'd naturally be looking out for him. D'you know Sutton's address?'

'No. Latchvale, I think.'

He keyed in a number. 'Extension thirty-seven, please . . . Andy? It's Tom Jones here. I need a favour, urgently . . . yeah. A villain in the West Midlands called Leonard Sutton . . . Latchvale, that's all I've got . . . hang on . . . What does he look like?' he called over to me.

I gave him a few details which he repeated, together with my number, before putting the phone down.

He looked at his watch. 'Half-past . . . listen, when he comes, let him inside, but then keep clear of him. So that he can't grab you. Got that? And let me do the talking.'

I nodded, then said, 'He's here.'

'OK, remember what I said.'

A moment later, the doorbell gave a long, continuous ring. I opened it and Polo strode inside. He seemed even more massive and intimidating than before, and I wondered how Jones could possibly . . .

'You got the stuff . . .?' He saw Jones . . . ''Oo the fuck're you?'

'My name's Jones. I'm from the Department of Health.'

He turned on me and, remembering, I took a couple of paces back.

'So you *did* squeal . . .'

'No, she didn't,' said Jones. 'She told the police two weeks ago and the information's only just got to me. I'm looking into these killings now — if there are any — and I don't need any help. Tell your boss that. You can also tell him I'll talk to him if he wants, but that's all. OK?'

Polo glared back at him for a moment, then said, 'I'll tell 'im. An' I'll take what I came for — the stuff Mr Sutton told me to get —'

'No, you won't. That's no concern of yours now. Tell your boss I'll talk to him.'

'*Mr Jones* —' I'd seen Polo's hand go into his pocket and now it came out with the knife.

'I said I'll take the stuff,' Polo said. 'Where is it?' As he spoke, the blade snapped out, but at the same time, to my amazement, a gun conjured itself into Jones's hand.

'Drop it.'

'You won't use that,' Polo said.

Jones said softly, 'Try me,' and both Polo and I believed him.

He lowered the knife. 'Aw right, but like I said, Mr Sutton'll be back —'

'I said, drop it.'

There was a pause, then the knife fell on the carpet. 'Out.'

Polo walked to the door and opened it.

'I'll remember you,' he said nasally, then pulled it closed behind him.

Jones went over to the window. I heard a car engine start, then he said, 'He's gone,' and put his gun away and picked up the knife. 'I shan't forget him, either. Remind me to —'

'D'you always carry a gun?' I burst out.

'Yes, usually,' he said quietly.

'Is that legal? Do the police —?'

'It's both legal and necessary — I'd have thought the necessity was illustrated just now —'

But by this time, I'd broken down again. He held me rather awkwardly as I sobbed on to his neck.

'Come and sit down. Over here.' He led me to the sofa, gently disengaging himself. 'I'll make you some tea or —'

'Whisky. Over there.'

He went over to the sideboard and picked up the bottle. 'You've been punishing this already, haven't you?'

'So I want to punish it some more,' I snapped. Irrationally, I felt annoyed with him for not holding me longer.

'OK.' He poured me a small tot and brought it over. 'When did you last eat?'

'I don't know. Yesterday. I'm not hungry.' I found a cigarette and lit it.

'I'm going to make you some tea,' he said. 'Is that the kitchen through there?'

'Yes.'

I heard him filling the kettle, and a few minutes later, I heard the toaster pop. A little while after that, he brought out a tray on which was a plate of beans on toast and some tea.

'Hardly cordon bleu, but it might help.' He held it out to me.

'I told you, I'm not hungry.'

'Try it.'

Of course, I was hungry, so much so that I asked for a repeat order.

'Better now?' he asked when I'd finished, and I nodded.

'D'you think you could try and tell me what's been going on now?' He had a distinct London accent, I noticed, a bit like Polo's, but not so nasal.

'Before I do that, could you tell me how . . . why you're involved?'

'Sure. As I said, I work for the Department of Health. It's my job to investigate . . . allegations like the one you've made.'

'So the Latchvale police contacted you?'

'Indirectly — which reminds me — I must apologize for the delay in contacting *you*, but your statement took some time to reach us.'

'I'm surprised it reached you at all,' I said, 'since I withdrew it about a week after I'd made it.'

'I know that. But when we saw it, we were impressed enough to want to look into it. Anyway, you'd better tell me your story.' As he said this, his eyes met mine. They were a clear hazel, I noticed, like my own. He brought out a small cheroot. 'I take it you don't mind if I smoke?'

'Hardly.' I pushed the ashtray towards him as he lit it.

His hair was a light brown as well; short, so that it looked like the fur of a small neat animal, a field vole — no, something more purposeful — a weasel perhaps, or a stoat. He was somewhere in his thirties.

He looked up again as if to say: Well, come on then.

'About five weeks ago,' I began hesitantly, 'I felt that . . . too many patients in my ward were dying when I hadn't expected them to. It does happen, but not this often. Anyway, I began to keep a record of them . . .'

It took me about half an hour, during which time his eyes never left my face, although he hardly spoke. When I told him about Sutton, my voice began to tremble again, and when I got to how Stephen had disbelieved me, I began to feel angry.

'Was a post-mortem done on any of the patients?' he asked, when I'd finished.

'No. They rarely are when patients die in hospital and the cause of death is obvious.'

'When did Mrs Sutton die?'

'Early yesterday morning.'

'I wonder if we could arrange for a PM on her . . .?' he said thoughtfully, then looked back at me. 'What proportion of patients would you normally expect to die in ITU?'

'It varies a lot, but about twenty per cent.'

'OK. Shall we have a look at these patients now, and your statistics.'

He read slowly through the notes I'd made for Miss Whittington, asking questions and making notes of his own. Some of the questions, I couldn't answer without the patient records that were on the computer. Then he got to my statistical analysis.

'Unless your basic data is inaccurate,' he said, 'I can see nothing wrong with this.'

'But Stephen — Dr Wall — told me I was wrong to have used percentages; besides which, I should have used the chi-square test, probably with Yates's correction.'

He laughed. 'That seems unnecessarily complicated. Unless your ward is full all the time, percentages are more accurate, and probability limits are perfectly adequate for your figures. But we can go through it again.'

He opened his briefcase and brought out a large calculator, and after checking over my basic data as much as we could, he input the figures.

'You were right,' he said at last. 'That number of deaths is clearly outside ninety-five per cent probability limits. Which, at the very least, leaves questions to be answered.' He sat back. 'So, what are we going to do about it?'

'You believe me, then?'

'Statistics don't lie.'

'But I thought there were *lies, damned lies, and statistics?*' I said, repeating Stephen.

'So there are, if you're a politician. Or a civil servant trying to screw cash out of the Treasury. But we simply want the truth. Any idea who's behind it?'

I shook my head. 'None.'

'Not even the wildest guess?'

'No.'

He let out a breath. 'So it's down to detective work and elimination. What shift are you working tomorrow?'

'I'm back on eight till four.'

'Is there anywhere where we can work and talk in private?'

'There's my office. Although people will wonder who you are, what you're doing.'

'That's not a problem. I've already made arrangements with your nursing officer, Miss Whittington, to spend some time with you. So far as she's concerned, I'm a finance auditor, collecting figures for the Department of Health.'

I shook my head slightly in bewilderment. 'How did you manage that?'

'My boss telephoned her boss. Told him we needed

some figures from the West Midlands urgently.' He'd taken out his wallet again, this time showing me a card which identified him as a finance auditor.

'So what do you want to do tomorrow?' I asked.

'Your ward's computerized, you said?'

'Yes.'

He took a breath and released it. 'The first thing we have to do is work out whether these killings are planned or random —'

'How do you mean?'

'Does our putative killer select each victim for some abstruse reason, or just take the opportunity to kill any patient when it occurs? Or have they poisoned some central supply of drugs? So I'll need all the information you can find about the patients who died, so that we can see if they have anything in common. The list of staff you got for Sutton — is it complete?'

'Yes, I think so.'

'D'you have records of all the staff shifts and work rotas over this period?'

'Yes, but not on computer.'

'That's all right, so long as you can get them together in a reasonably coherent form. What I need to do tomorrow is to get an idea how ITU functions — as would a real auditor — and then to meet as many of the staff as possible. Also, I'll have to visit any other wards and departments connected with yours — you did say that two of the dead patients had been transferred to the Coronary Care ward, didn't you? Can we do all that, d'you think?'

'It might be difficult in one day. It would make it easier if we left chasing up the staff rotas till the weekend —'

I was interrupted by the phone.

'Hello?'

'Sister Farewell? It's Miss Whittington here.'

'Oh, hello, Miss Whittington.'

'I hope I haven't disturbed you. I understand you've been on night duty.'

'No, you haven't disturbed me.'

'Good. The reason I'm ringing is that I've had a rather curious request from the Department of Health. They've sent an auditor here to look into the relationships between ITU and other departments.'

'Oh?'

'Yes. I understand you'll be back tomorrow morning. Will you be able to spare him any time then?'

'Er — I think so, yes.'

'Good. But, Sister, I'd like you to keep me informed about what questions he asks, what it is he wants to know.'

'Of course, Miss Whittington.'

She hesitated . . . 'There was one other thing, Sister . . .'

'Yes?'

I heard her take a breath. 'Dr Wall tells me he thinks you've been under an inordinate amount of stress

86

recently — something that had already occurred to me, you may remember . . .'

I didn't hear the rest. You *bastard*! I thought furiously. How could you?

I heard myself agreeing that we should discuss it, then replaced the receiver.

'What's the problem?' Jones asked, but before I could reply, the phone went again.

'For you,' I said, holding it out to him.

'Hello? Oh, hello, Andy . . . hang on a minute while I find a pen . . .'

I leaned back into the sofa while he found pen and paper and closed my eyes. I don't know whether it was the sleepless nights, the release of tension after Polo's visit or Stephen's treachery, but a savage pain started pulsing behind my eyes and I wanted nothing more than to forget everything and sink into my bed . . .

The drone of his voice stopped and I realized he'd been speaking to me.

'I'm sorry?'

'I said, is there any reason why we shouldn't go in now and get the patient records from the computer? So I could make a start on them.'

'Yes, there is.' The words came with difficulty. 'I can't remember when I last felt this awful. Also, it would look odd. I'm not expected until tomorrow morning.'

'You might have a point there — we don't want to alert the person we're after. Listen, I'm sorry you feel so rough, but it would help if you could answer a few more questions before I go.'

'*Go?*' Fear banished the pain for a moment and I sat up. 'Mr Jones, I'd . . . I rather assumed you'd stay — for tonight, anyway. Sutton isn't going to be very pleased with me after Polo's told him what's happened.'

'Stay here, you mean?'

'If you think your reputation could stand it. I do have a spare room.'

'All right,' he said after a moment, not really liking it. 'I'll need to collect some things from my hotel, though. And let my wife know where I am.'

I didn't like the idea of being left alone at all, so I went with him to his hotel while he collected a few things, although I can't remember much about the journey.

When we got back, he started asking more questions about the patients on my notes, but I was too tired to make much sense, and after a while, he gave up.

'Can I use your phone?' he asked. 'I want to find out about a PM on Mrs Sutton, among other things.'

'Help yourself.'

I staggered away upstairs before he could think of anything else, took a couple of paracetamols and went to bed.

Strangely enough, I didn't sleep immediately. The pain in my head slowly diminished to a manageable point in the middle of my brow, and all the while, I was aware of Jones's voice droning away on the phone downstairs. It was oddly comforting.

*

I was awoken by a persistent tapping. Didn't realize it was from my door until he said, 'Sister, I need to speak to you. It's important.'

'What time is it?'

'Half-past eight.'

I'd slept for eight hours, although it didn't feel like it.

'What's the matter?'

'I'll tell you when you come down. Would you like a coffee?'

'All right.'

I dragged on some clothes and splashed some water on to my face before going down. He was sitting on the sofa, smoking a cheroot. Two mugs of coffee were on the table in front of him.

'What's the problem?' I looked for my cigarettes, then realized I didn't want one.

'A problem is exactly what we've got,' he said deliberately.

'Well?' I sat on the sofa beside him and took a mouthful of coffee.

'I've been on the phone to my boss for most of the day — which reminds me, I'll have to reimburse you for that . . .'

'I wish you'd get to the point.'

'All right.'

It occurred to me that he really was worried about something.

'While my boss accepts my judgement that there probably have been killings at your hospital, he says we need some hard evidence.'

The coffee had begun to clear my head. 'You said something earlier about arranging a PM on Mrs Sutton.'

'Indeed I did. Unfortunately, her funeral's tomorrow morning.'

'Can't it be delayed?'

'It could, yes, but my boss would prefer to avoid that.'

'But I can't see —'

'Listen. You've already been to the police and told them people were being murdered on your ward. Then you went back and told them it was all a mistake —'

'But you know why I —'

'Yes, but it doesn't alter the fact that you withdrew your allegation, and that a death certificate's been signed for Mrs Sutton. To get a PM done now, we'd have to convince the coroner, and that would take some doing.'

'But surely your department could —'

'It could be done, yes, but what d'you think Sutton's feelings would be at this stage? Especially if the PM didn't find anything.'

'But I thought you said you believed me.'

'I said that there was nothing wrong with your analysis and that it needed investigating.'

I slumped forward. 'So what can we do about it?'

'Mrs Sutton's body's still in the hospital mortuary. We go and get a blood sample from it ourselves — tonight.'

Chapter 9

'You're out of your mind.' I said it quite calmly.

'No,' he said equally calmly. 'My boss told me that if we really couldn't do it, he'd try and get it done officially. But the news would get out — there's no way we could stop it. And it could be potentially disastrous for you — not to mention your career.'

'But what can a blood sample tell us? There should be a complete PM . . .'

'In ideal circumstances, yes. But if she was murdered, it has to be by drugs. You were there when she died, weren't you?'

I nodded reluctantly.

'So whatever it was that killed her should still be in her bloodstream.'

He looked at me steadily. He was right.

I needed that cigarette badly now. I lit it and blew smoke. 'How would we get in?'

'I have keys that would do it.'

'I don't even know whether you can get blood from a corpse,' I said wildly. Not true, I remembered.

'D'you think I like it any more than you?' he snarled. 'It's for your sake, dammit!'

Looking at him, I could see that he really was as unhappy as me about it.

'All right!' I snapped. 'I think it may be possible,' I went on slowly. 'I seem to remember that blood doesn't clot in a body, it just sinks.'

'D'you know where the mortuary is?'

I nodded.

'Have you ever been inside?'

'Yes — years ago.'

'What's the security like?'

'Er — it's kept locked, obviously. And there's an intercom.'

'It's not manned at night?'

'I don't think so. I'm almost certain it isn't.'

'Intruder alarms?'

'Er — I don't know.'

He swallowed. 'Well, we'll find out, won't we?'

*

An hour later. I'd dressed in my uniform and we went in my car — we'd be less conspicuous, he said. He drove.

I went into ITU to collect the necessary equipment. There was no one in the Duty Room. I opened a cupboard, found a syringe, needles.

'Jo?'

I turned.

'Oh, hello, Teresa.' Surely she would notice the unnecessary uniform, hear the tremor in my voice. 'Just checking we've got some stuff I need tomorrow for a demonstration. Everything all right?'

'Fine. How about you? I heard you had a pretty grim time.'

'Yes. Fine now, thanks.'

I took the stuff into my office and waited till she was busy before thrusting it into my handbag. Fiddled around a bit more before going.

'Bye, Teresa.'

'Night, Jo.'

'Got everything?' asked Jones as I got back into the car.

I nodded. 'Yes.'

'You were a long time.'

'Ran into someone. Do we take the car?' St Chad's was an old hospital and covered a large area.

'No, we'll leave it here and walk.'

Our footsteps were unnaturally loud. No one was about, but I felt painfully conspicuous — what possible legitimate reason could we have for being here? We were approaching the boiler house . . .

'It's the next building along,' I said quietly.

'We'll go past it and round the back,' he said.

There was a light outside the front. We walked past, then, without looking round, turned into the shadows on the far side. It was like walking into blindness.

He took out a pencil torch and flashed it — I bumped into him to avoid a drain.

We turned into the passage at the back. Found the door. He shone the light around it.

'No sign of an alarm neutralizer,' he murmured, handing me the torch. 'You'll have to hold this for me.'

He brought out a bunch of keys. I shone the pencil beam on to the lock. He inserted one of them; tried moving it about before withdrawing it.

I'd just begun to think we weren't going to do it when the fourth key turned. He pushed the door a little way and listened before pushing it open. He put the keys away and took the torch from me. We went in and he shut the door. The faint, nutty smell of formaldehyde clamped on to my nostrils.

He said, 'Where's the front door?'

'Straight up there.' I pointed.

Our shoes clacked on the tiled floor; echoed on the tiled walls. Past the marble slabs of the post-mortem theatre; past the humming units of the refrigerated body store.

He shone his torch on to the front door, found a bolt and pushed it across.

'Now,' he said. 'Let's find her, shall we?' His own voice held a slight tremor, I noticed.

He led the way back to the body store.

'Shall we put the lights on?' I asked.

'No. Might get somebody wondering.'

He fiddled with the torch and the light strengthened.

'Shine it up there,' I said, pointing to the stainless steel refrigerator doors. 'The names should be there.'

There were four doors in a row, four names on each . . .

Underhill, Finch, Prescott, Williams . . .

Next door.

Lynch, Newman, *Sutton*.

He reached up and pulled the handle . . . it clicked and the door swung open.

The cadavers were stacked, each on a metal tray, each wrapped in a sheet, the head towards us. She was the third one down; approximately thigh height.

'These just slide out, don't they?' he said.

'Yes, but they're not —'

Before I could stop him, he'd grasped the handle at the front of the tray and pulled it out . . . and the tray and body fell on to the floor with an orchestral crash . . .

I gazed at him, appalled. 'How *could* you . . .?' was all I could find to say to him.

He was on his knees, lifting and straightening the body back on the tray.

'Check that it's her first,' he said.

'But we can't . . . oh no . . .'

'*Do it!*'

He'd pulled out a penknife and cut the cord tying the sheet. It fell away to reveal the blonde hair and still, slack face of Mrs Sutton. Through everything, I observed that rigor mortis had passed off.

'We'll be caught,' I said. 'Someone must have heard us.'

'Not necessarily. And even if they did, we've got at least five minutes. The arm?'

I nodded vacantly.

'Get your equipment out.'

I knelt, opened my bag, took out the syringe and stripped the plastic covering away into my pocket. Found and fitted a needle. The tiles were cold on my knees.

He'd pulled the calico shroud up her arm. I felt in the cubital fossa for a vein . . . couldn't find one . . . of course not — no blood pressure . . .

I swallowed, inserted the needle into the cold flesh, pulled on the plunger . . . nothing. Pushed the needle deeper, tried again, felt sick. Still nothing.

'I — I can't.'

'Keep trying,' he said urgently.

'Hold the bloody torch still then, will you!'

Think. Where would it be?

I pulled the needle out and tried again, a little to one side.

Nothing.

Deeper, and my fingers felt the faintest pop as the needle found a vein . . .

Drew on the plunger, and about a mil of fluid trickled into the syringe . . . stopped.

'We need more than that,' he said. 'Five mil.'

'I *know*!'

I reached up the arm as far as the coarse material of the shroud, squeezed, my fingers sinking into the cold flesh; repeated it, lower down. Pulled the plunger again . . . and again, there was a trickle of fluid.

'We still need more,' he said urgently.

At that moment, we heard the wail of a siren, close, inside the hospital . . .

Our eyes met . . .

'Ambulance?' he said.

'Too close — they go the other way.'

We were on our feet.

'What about . . .?' I looked down at Mrs Sutton.

'No time. Get that syringe away.'

It was in my hand. I thrust it, needle still in place, into my bag. He flicked the sleeve of the shroud back, shone the torch around, picked up the lid of the needle container . . . the siren grew nearer, we ran . . .

He opened the back door, held it for me, pulled it shut as we heard the police car pull up at the front.

'Which way?' he whispered.

'*I* don't know.'

I ran from the building on to the grass towards the back of the boiler house, hoping I wouldn't trip; heard him behind me . . . then our feet hit the tarmac . . . I reached the corner, turned . . .

He grabbed my arm.

'Slow down. Don't attract attention. Which way's the car?'

'Round here.'

There was enough light to find our way along behind the boiler house and back to the road.

'It's over there. We'll have to cross over.'

'Let's do it now.'

He put his arm round me as we stepped into the light. The revolving blue from the police car made a grimace of his smile. His eyes flicked back up the road.

'What's happening?' I asked, through my own false smile.

'Police car. Can't see any police. They must be inside, or round the back.'

We came to a covered way. He left his arm round me.

'Down here,' I said, and we turned. Passed a couple of nurses who were laughing at something. Turned again and a moment later, found my car.

'You drive,' he said, handing me the keys.

'Why?'

'It'll look better.'

My trembling hands unlocked the car and we got

in. I put my bag on the back seat and started the engine. Switched on the lights, turned and made for the entrance . . .

A policeman in a fluorescent jacket stepped out and flagged us down. I stopped, wound down the window. His eyes took in my uniform.

'Good evening. We've had a report of an intruder. Do you have any identification, please?'

'Will this do?' I unpinned my identity badge and handed it to him.

'Sister Farewell.' He looked up. 'Is this your car?'

'Yes, it is.'

'Could you repeat the registration number, please?'

I did so.

'And your name, sir?' He shone the torch past me on to Jones.

'Tom Jones.' He took out his driving licence and held it out. 'I'm a — a friend of Miss Farewell's.'

The policeman smiled. 'Thank you, sir.' He shone his torch into the back — my heart stopped when I remembered my bag, but he said, 'I don't think we need trouble you any more. Good night.'

'Night,' said Jones.

Chapter 10

Neither of us spoke until we were out of sight of the police, then I said through my teeth, 'Don't ever do anything like that to me again.'

'I'm sorry. I thought it pulled out like a drawer. I didn't realize it would do that.'

We pulled up at the lights. I said, 'What if we left something behind?'

'We didn't.'

'How d'you know? What about fingerprints?'

'D'you really think they're going to fingerprint the entire hospital?'

'They're going to have to do something.'

'Why are they? Think about it. No damage was done and a full-scale investigation would only upset the relatives. They'll say very little and do very little.'

The lights changed and I pulled away.

'It was horrible,' I said.

'I didn't exactly enjoy it myself.'

'I want a bath as soon as I get back.'

We didn't say any more until we arrived. I locked the car.

He was waiting for me at the front door. Inside, he said, 'Why don't you put the sample in the fridge, then you can have your bath?'

I transferred it from the syringe into the bottle. There were barely two mils.

'Will it be enough?' I asked.

He shrugged, his face pale. 'Pack it, and I'll get it on to Red Star tomorrow.'

I did so and put the package in the fridge, then poured myself a strong whisky and lit a cigarette. He'd already helped himself and had a cheroot going.

I swallowed the whisky, but the uncleanness seemed to be clinging to my fingers.

'Why don't you have your bath?' he said.

'You know the worst of it?' I burst out. 'It was treating her like that. It was disrespect, a violation. She's still a person; still entitled to respect.'

'Yes. But don't you think we also owe it to her to find her killer? Isn't that respect?' He swallowed his own drink. 'I think I'll have a bath myself after you.'

I went up and put all my clothes in the dirty washing before climbing into the hot water.

*

The alarm woke me at seven the next morning. Amazingly, I'd slept without much trouble, but the whisky might have had something to do with that. I lay in bed for a few minutes, trying to sort things out in my mind before getting up and going to the bathroom.

Actually, I didn't feel too bad. The worst of the unclean feeling had gone, and the mirror told me the swellings on my face had almost gone, too. I had a quick wash, put on my uniform and went downstairs.

Jones, who'd elected to sleep on the sofa, seemed to be still asleep, but his eyes flicked open as I went past him.

'Sleep all right?' I asked.

'Fine, thanks. You?'

'Not bad, considering.'

He waited until I'd gone into the kitchen, then went up to the bathroom himself.

I got myself some cereal and coffee. He came down after about fifteen minutes in a dark suit and tie.

'You're looking very spruce, Mr Jones,' I told him.

'All part of the image of the minor government official,' he informed me gravely. 'And it's Tom. At least, white there's no one else about,' he added.

I grinned. 'And I'm Jo. D'you want any breakfast?'

'Cereal'll be fine, thanks.'

'Coffee?'

'Please.'

'So how do we plan today, Tom?' I asked after a few minutes.

He swallowed a mouthful of cereal.

'You go into work normally; I'll take the package to the station and probably get in half an hour after you. I'll introduce myself, then you can start showing me around. Try and introduce me to everyone we come across — without being ridiculous about it. And as you do, try to say what their job is as well as their name — again, without going over the top. After that, we'll need to discuss the next step. Reasonable so far?'

'Yes,' I said. 'There's a consultant's ward round at nine. D'you want to see that?'

'Yes, in that it'll help show me who's who.'

'All right. I'd better go.'

I went upstairs, brushed my teeth, put on some warpaint and left.

*

There was no sign of any police at the hospital. The whole of the previous evening was beginning to seem surreal, as though it hadn't happened.

'Hello, stranger,' said James when I got in. 'You had fun and games, so I hear.'

'You could call it that,' I said coldly, irritated by his

tone. He meant no harm, but his insensitivity could be irksome sometimes.

'Hello,' said Emma as I went into the Duty Room. 'We heard about what happened to you. Are you feeling better now?'

'I wouldn't have blamed you for having a couple of days off,' said Viv.

'The call of duty was too strong,' I said, thinking: You don't know the tenth of it.

'Did Miss Whittington phone you about Mr Jones, the auditor who dropped in yesterday?' Viv continued.

'Yes, she did. Which reminds me — I'll probably need to spend most of the day with him. Could you do the ward round, please, Viv?'

Her eyes gleamed. 'Sure.'

'What's he like?' I asked mendaciously. 'Mr Jones?'

'The auditor?' said James, who'd just come in, obviously unchastened. 'Not your type at all.'

'I didn't realize you knew me so —' I began coolly, but then Stephen came in.

'Hello, Jo,' he said, smiling. 'Are you feeling better now?'

'Yes, thank you.' My heart, which had skipped a beat, settled into a faster rhythm.

'Good. Has Viv brought you up to date yet?'

'She was about to.'

'Only, I'm a bit worried about Mr Whitaker . . .'

His tone, his whole demeanour, was completely

natural — neutral, as though nothing had happened between us, and it was only with an effort I could bring myself to discuss the various patients with him. But I did, and was still doing so when there was an apologetic cough behind us at the door. Tom Jones had arrived.

'Sister Farewell?' he said.

It was hard not to grin at him.

'Mr Jones, I presume.' I held out a hand. 'Do come in. These good people have been telling me all about you.'

'Oh?' he said, almost nervously.

Stephen was staring at him curiously. I said, 'You obviously met some of them yesterday, but I'll introduce you anyway. This is Dr Wall, senior registrar . . .'

'Pleased to meet you,' he said eagerly, offering a hand.

He simply wasn't the same man. He'd somehow turned himself into, well, a minor government official, to use his own words — bland and eager to please almost to the point of obsequiousness.

'Exactly what sort of information is it you're looking for?' Stephen was asking him.

'Patient/staff ratios, types of staff, success rates, and perhaps most importantly, how the work of this unit interfaces with the work of other units and departments in this hospital.'

'Why?' Stephen demanded, then smiled. 'You're not planning to close us down, are you?'

'Oh no, nothing like that, I assure you. The government wants to know how hospital departments interface, so as to ascertain whether there are savings that could be made in that area.'

Masterly, I thought. Believable for its very vapidity.

'I see,' said Stephen. 'Well, I hope —'

'Telephone, Dr Wall,' said James behind him and he excused himself.

'This is Viv Aldridge, nursing sister,' I said, continuing with the introductions. 'And James Croxall and Emma Riley, staff nurses.' He nodded pleasantly to each of them.

'How long will you be here, Mr Jones?' asked Viv.

'A few days at the most. Please don't mind me. Just carry on working as you would normally.'

He'd allowed his London accent to become more marked; at the same time carefully enunciating his Hs and Ts, sounding very much the working-class boy made good. It certainly made him seem harmless.

The doorway darkened and I looked up to see Miss Whittington.

'Good morning, Sister, Mr Jones. You've managed to find each other, then?'

'Yes, indeed,' said Jones.

'Good. Perhaps we could go into your office for a few moments.'

'Certainly, Miss Whittington.' My, we *are* all being polite today, I thought, glad she wouldn't be able to bring up the subject of the 'stress' I'd been under.

Once inside, I listened respectfully while she told me what I already knew, viz, the ostensible reason for Mr Jones's visit, fishing as she did for any hidden motive that might affect her. I nodded and said 'yes' in the right places, reflecting that it must be her way of keeping on top of things.

After she'd gone, he said quietly, 'Is she always like that?'

'Yes. I sometimes wonder whether she's slightly paranoid.'

'She's said nothing more to you about the dead patients?'

'No. Not since a few days after I first spoke to her.' I glanced up at the clock. 'If I'm to show you any of the ward before the round, we'd better start now.'

'All right.' He stood up. 'Has anything been said about last night?'

'Nothing.'

I took him to the gowning lobby, where he put on the gown I handed him without any help.

'You've done this before,' I remarked.

'Yes.'

Inside, Emma was at the nurses' station, while James, Armitage and Pete Hadley were sitting with patients. Susan was taking blood from another.

I glanced at the clock. A quarter-to.

'Everything ready for the round?' I asked Emma.

'Yes.' She nodded vigorously.

'No problems?'

'None.'

I took him round the ward, telling him quietly what was wrong with each patient before explaining the functions of the monitors and other bedside equipment, and introducing him to Armitage, Hadley and Susan. They all looked slightly surprised. I don't usually introduce visitors to them.

'What are these rooms, Sister?' He pointed to the isolation rooms and I explained.

'The patients in these two are recovering from renal transplant. They're on immunosuppressive drugs, which means they're —'

'They're susceptible to infection,' he finished for me.

'That's right.' I acknowledged a wave from Sophie Marsh who was sitting with one of them.

'How long will they have to stay there?' he asked.

'Until the transplant's taken and the immunosuppressives can be reduced. Could be days or weeks.'

'Who's in this room?' He pointed to the third.

I glanced round before saying in a low voice, 'That patient died yesterday in another ward. He's being kept on life support for organ donation.'

'A rather morbid contradiction in terms. A dead patient on life support.'

'You know what I mean.'

'How long will he stay there?'

'Until an organ match is found. Then he'll be moved to the site of the transplant operation.'

Then there was a stir and the whole ward seemed to come to attention as Mr Chorley and his retinue filed in.

'The ward round,' I said.

Chapter 11

We watched as they approached the first bed and Viv explained something to Mr Chorley. She was looking very much at home, I observed a trifle sourly.

'Can you tell me their names?' Tom said quietly.

'The man talking now, that's Mr Chorley, the consultant. Stephen Wall, you met. The others are Ian Hadmore, senior house officer, Paul Ridware and Jill Newton, house officers.' I went on to explain how the round was conducted.

'Do any of them carry out invasive treatments on the patients?'

'Mr Chorley, very rarely. The others, yes, although it varies.'

We watched a little longer, then he said he'd seen enough for the moment, we de-gowned and I showed him round the rest of the unit.

We'd seen the pantry and sterile preparation room, and were in the relatives' room, which was empty at the moment. He said, 'I noticed that a lot of the patients had a nurse actually sitting with them — is that usually the case?'

'Much more so than in an ordinary ward. Each patient has a nurse with them at least half the time.'

'Is it always the same nurse?'

'Usually, although not necessarily. For instance . . .' I told him about Emma and Mr Phillips.

'So the same nurse would also always give the patient an injection, or any other such treatment?'

'Same answer — usually, but not necessarily.'

He thought for a moment. 'So wouldn't that make it rather difficult for a nurse, or a doctor, to just go up to a patient and say: *It's time for your such-and-such, Mr Bloggs*, and inject him with something that killed him?'

It was my turn to think.

'It would make it more difficult, yes. But it would depend on who they were, on their authority and how well they knew the system.'

'But surely it would be risky? I mean, if Mr Bloggs was your patient, and you went in and saw another nurse giving him an injection, wouldn't you want to know why?'

'Yes, but if they said: *Because Dr Brown told me to*, that would answer it.'

'Still too risky. Too easily checked.'

'I suppose so . . .'

'We're looking for somebody, or something, that would obviate that risk.' He took a breath. 'Where d'you keep your fluids for drips and suchlike?'

'In the store, just across the corridor.'

That was empty as well. I showed him the drip sets, which were sealed in tough plastic bags.

'Are these ever opened in here?' he asked.

I shook my head. 'Each bag contains four sets, so we take two or three bags at a time into the ward and open them there.'

'But it would be quite easy for a doctor, or nurse, to smuggle an unused set out of the ward?'

'Er — yes, I suppose it would. But surely it would be obvious if one had been tampered with?'

'Would it? Can I open one of these?' Without waiting for an answer, he took out his penknife, slit one of the bags open and pulled out a set. 'You lift the label so,' he said, gently sliding the point of the knife underneath the label on the plastic pack and twisting the blade. 'You inject your poison, then stick the label back down with glue. Who would know?'

I shook my head. 'Where did you learn that?'

He smiled, rather sadly. 'I'll tell you some other time.'

'You think that's how it was done?'

'It's a possibility. It would certainly overcome the problem of being spotted giving an illicit injection.'

'But how would the killer know which patient was going to —? Oh . . . I see what you meant now about whether the killings are planned or random. But how are we going to work out which?'

'The patient records on computer might help us there. You did say all treatments are recorded?'

'That's right.'

'Shall we go and look at them?'

'If you like. I thought you said yesterday you wanted to see the Coronary Care ward?'

'I did, didn't I? Shall we do that quickly first?'

Coronary Care is a bit more like most hospital wards —about twenty patients, with a much lower staff/patient ratio, not so much high-tech equipment and no gowning air-lock. Mr Chorley and his caravan had just started their round there.

I introduced Tom to the sister in charge, quickly pointed out the ward's features, then we returned to ITU.

'And that's where a patient would be transferred when their condition had improved in ITU?' he said when we were in the corridor.

'Yes. Or perhaps the Medical ward.'

He lowered his voice. 'Easier to kill someone in there, I'd have thought. Not so many nosey nurses to worry about.'

'True.'

'And yet only two of your group of eight died there. I wonder why? Opportunity? Something else we haven't thought of?'

'I don't know,' I said slowly. 'Although, because of its nature, there are more deaths anyway in ITU than in other wards . . .'

'So a sudden death wouldn't be so unexpected . . .' he said. 'Like the wood and the trees. It took half a dozen sudden deaths before you spotted anything, and even then, nobody else believed you.'

We arrived at ITU and went through to my office. Viv was in the Duty Room.

'Everything go all right?' I asked her.

'No problem. I enjoyed it.' She grinned. 'How long did you say you'd be here, Mr Jones?'

'Mm? Oh, only a few days.'

'There's no rush. Don't hurry on my account.'

'Oh, I wouldn't do that,' he said seriously. Viv made a face as we went into my office.

As soon as I closed the door, he said, 'Is it reasonably soundproof in here?'

'Reasonably. If we keep our voices down.'

'Are we likely to be disturbed?'

'It's a possibility, since I am supposed to be the sister in charge. Although people usually knock when they see my door's closed.'

'Then shall we have a look at the record of one of

the patients who died?' He indicated the computer terminal. 'If anyone does come in, you're just showing me how the system works.'

I keyed in my password and called up the patient record system, then tapped in HANBURY, PAUL.

'You certainly have plenty of information on them,' he said, over my shoulder. 'Can you print that one out?'

'Now?'

'Why not? We'll be needing copies of them.'

I pressed the right keys, but nothing happened, so I went over to the printer and switched it off and on again. Nothing.

'Let me have a look,' he said.

He fiddled with it for a moment, then switched it off and undid something at the back.

'Fuse.' He held it up. 'D'you have a spare?'

'Somewhere.' I found one in a drawer and he fitted it. Then I began printing all the files on the patients I suspected had been murdered.

I'd just started on the last — Mrs Sutton — when there was a knock on the door and Viv came in. She was holding a printout.

'Is this yours?' she asked. 'Patient record on Paul Hanbury. No one out there will admit to it.'

I felt myself colouring. 'It's ours,' I said, holding my hand out. 'I was showing Mr Jones the patient record system and the printer wasn't working. It must have defaulted to the one out there.'

She gave it to me, glancing over at the screen as she did.

'Thank you, Viv,' I said.

'You're welcome.' She went out, pulling the door to behind her.

'I'm sorry about that,' I said quietly.

He moved over to the door and looked out through the glass panel.

'Probably doesn't matter,' he said. 'Who's the girl over there?'

I moved beside him. He was looking at Sophie, who was talking to Viv.

'Sophie Marsh. She's the staff nurse we saw earlier in with the renal transplant patient. Why?'

'I remember her now. She's the only one I couldn't place.'

The Duty Room was quite busy. Susan was replenishing her tray with sample bottles, while Armitage was hanging round looking superfluous. Pretty Jill Newton was talking animatedly to Stephen, and as I watched, I felt a sharp spurt of jealousy. Almost as though he'd felt it too, Stephen looked up at me. I turned away.

Tom was looking at me as well. After a pause, he said, 'What I'd really like to do now is go over these printouts with you in detail. We can't do it here. Is there a library, or somewhere like that we could use?'

'Not really, if we want to talk.' I thought for a

moment. 'I'm afraid the best I can suggest is that we go back to my house for lunch.' I looked up at the clock. It was just after eleven. 'And I can't really do that for another hour,' I said.

'That's all right. I'll go and study these on my own for a bit. Give you a chance to catch up on some paperwork or something.'

I told him how to get to the library, then did as he suggested and attacked some of the paperwork that had accumulated during my absence. My mind was so full that it was a while before I could get into it, and no sooner than I had than a voice behind me said, 'Excuse me, Sister . . .'

I jumped as though from an electric shock and swiv-elled round to see the plain, plaintive features of Helen Armitage.

'Please, don't do that, Nurse Armitage,' I said. 'You frightened the life out of me.'

'I'm sorry, Sister. Your door was open.'

So it was.

'How can I help you?'

'Could I have an overtime form, please?'

'Aren't there any in the Duty Room?'

'I couldn't see any.'

I gave her a handful. 'Take one for yourself and leave the rest out there.'

'Thank you, Sister.'

I shouldn't have jumped like that, I thought after

she'd gone. Nerves. I hoped very much that Tom would find the killer soon.

Almost as though he'd heard me through some form of ESP, he came in and shut the door.

'I think I've spotted something,' he said.

Chapter 12

'Well? What is it?' I asked eagerly.

He tapped the pile of printouts. 'With the exception of Mrs Sutton, every one of these patients was not only carrying an organ donor card, but also had their organs transplanted.'

The disappointment must have shown in my face.

'Well, wouldn't you have said that was unusual?' he demanded.

'Not in this hospital, no.'

'But seven out of eight, compared with the national average . . .?'

'Miss Shenstone, who's in charge of the Transplant Department here, was one of the founding fathers — mothers, I should say — of transplant surgery back in the 'sixties, and St Chad's has always had a policy of trying to recover every organ we can. So seven out of eight is pretty good, but not a rarity.'

'You're missing my point. These seven all carried donor cards. What's the national average of that — twenty-five, thirty per cent?'

'There's been an aggressive advertising campaign in this area. Obviously, it's working.'

'I can't believe it's working that well. It needs looking into.'

'What are you trying to suggest?' I demanded. 'That these people were killed for their organs? That's the most ridic —'

'Keep your voice down,' he hissed, looking round. Viv and Emma were in the Duty Room. 'I said it needed looking into, that's all.'

'I can't believe any doctor could be that callous,' I went on in a lower tone. 'Especially Miss Shenstone. She's regarded as a near saint in some quarters . . .'

'All right,' he said quietly. 'Arrange for me to meet her.'

'I can't do that . . .'

'Why not? My brief is to look at interfaces between departments — remember? And considering the occupants of your three side rooms, I'd say ITU and Transplant have a considerable interface, wouldn't you? Give her a try now, she can only say no.'

I thought quickly. I *had* been told to cooperate with him, and he was right, there was an 'interface'. And she could only say no. I picked up the phone.

'You're lucky,' I said thirty seconds later. 'Very. She says if we're there at two, she can give us ten minutes. And stop smirking,' I snapped.

*

We drove back to my house in his car, an elderly, but beautifully restored Mini-Cooper, since he thought it would seem natural enough for us to go to lunch together. He was a careful, sensual driver. I asked him whether he'd found anything else on the printouts. No, he said, nothing concrete yet, but he'd be able to use them, and the staff rota sheets I was going to find to indicate the most likely suspects.

I made some cheese and salad sandwiches while he phoned the Poisons Unit at Guy's in London to check whether the sample had arrived.

'Well?' I said, as I handed him his sandwiches.

'They've got the sample all right, but there's not enough, especially as we ought to keep some of it as evidence. They want us to think about which are the most likely agents our killer would have used, so that they can start with those. You're the nurse, Jo. Any ideas?' He took a bite of his sandwich.

'I suppose the most obvious would be potassium chloride,' I said after swallowing my mouthful. 'D'you remember that mercy killing by a consultant in Hants a couple of years ago? His patient was an old lady who was in so much pain from rheumatoid arthritis that even massive doses of heroin wouldn't suppress it. She begged him to put her out of her misery and he injected two ampoules of the concentrate, which killed her.'

'And that was from heart failure?'

'Yes. An excessive blood—potassium level causes muscle debility, and that kind of dose leads to heart block and failure.'

'But if I remember rightly, she died more or less instantaneously. I can't imagine our killer risking that happening, not eight times. If they did, they'll be easy to spot.'

'If the injection were subcutaneous,' I said slowly, 'or intramuscular, the effect would be delayed.'

'By how long?'

'I'm not sure in the case of concentrated potassium chloride, but it could be two or three hours.'

'Is it easy to get hold of?'

'I think you can buy it in a chemist's. Nothing simpler in a hospital.'

'Would it show up on post-mortem?'

I hesitated. 'I think a large dose would, although the body naturally contains a certain amount.'

'So potassium chloride's a possibility.' He made a note in his book. 'What about the nurse who killed those children with insulin?'

'Yes,' I said grimly. 'In Thatchbury. And she tried all sorts of methods, including potassium chloride as well as suffocation and air embolism. That's injecting an intravenous bubble of air,' I added in response to his quizzical look.

'So that does actually work, then?'

'It's a bit of an old chestnut really, since you have to inject a hell of a lot, at least a hundred mil. In her case, she didn't inject enough, and it only made the victim ill.'

'So probably not that, then.' He made another note. 'You mentioned suffocation — is that really possible?'

'Certainly, if the patient's unconscious. You pinch the nose and put your hand over their mouth.'

'But I imagine it would be pretty obvious if you were seen doing it? Which would be quite likely in ITU.'

'Yes, and it would also cause the alarm to go off when the heart stopped — if the patient were connected to a monitor.'

'That's a point,' he said. 'How many of them were connected to monitors at the time they died?'

We went through the printouts while we finished our sandwiches. Peters hadn't been on a monitor, of course, nor Mr Thorpe or Mr Goldman, who'd both been transferred to Coronary Care. The others all had, which didn't tell us very much.

'Shall I make some coffee?' I said, and got up without waiting for an answer.

'Let's get back to insulin,' Tom said as I handed him a mug a few minutes later. 'How did they find out that insulin was the agent used in the Thatchbury cases?'

'A post-mortem on one of the victims.'

'So it's detectable on PM.' He made another note. 'How does it cause heart failure? I only know it as the stuff diabetics use.'

'It's a hormone which controls the amount of sugar released into the blood. Diabetics can't make it, so they have too much sugar. Conversely, if you have an excess of insulin, the blood's starved of sugar and that leads to heart failure.'

'How long does it take to work? After you've injected it.'

'It varies. Soluble insulin acts in a minimum of thirty minutes, but it can take up to several hours.'

'And if you injected it intramuscularly . . .?'

'It would presumably take longer — I don't know. But, Tom, the killer wouldn't have to do that, since there are delayed action forms of insulin.'

He groaned. 'What are they and how long do they take to work?'

'Er — well, there's insulin zinc, which takes a bit longer, and there's protamine zinc insulin, or PZI, which takes longer still.'

He was busily scribbling. 'How much longer?'

'I'll have to look that up when we get back. It's a long time, though.'

'OK. So insulin's a strong possibility.' He looked up. 'Are all these various forms easily available?'

'Yes, they're just kept in a fridge.'

'I wonder if these could be copycat killings,' he mused. 'Should we be looking for a nurse with a similar sort of personality defect to the one in Thatchbury?'

'She had Munchausen's syndrome, and also Munchausen's syndrome by proxy.'

'Which means?'

'In the former, you gain attention by inventing symptoms of illness in yourself; in the latter, you bring about symptoms in those under your care. She had both. Also, she was inadequate.'

'Is there anyone like that on ITU?'

'Not that I can think of at the moment.'

'We'll bear it in mind.' He made another note. 'What other drugs are there which affect the heart?'

'Well, there's digitalin, or digoxin, which is used to reduce blood pressure. Reduce it enough, and you've got heart failure. Although it's usually given by mouth rather than by injection.'

'But it can be injected?'

'Yes.'

'Is it easily available?'

'We keep it locked away, although nothing like so securely as we do controlled drugs.'

'So a nurse or a doctor could lay their hands on some if they wanted to?'

'Yes, although not as easily as insulin.'

'D'you know how long it takes to work?'

'I'll check when we get back.'

'Is there anything else?'

'The other heart regulators we use are tenoret and propanolol, but they're administered orally.'

He stopped writing and looked at me. 'We've been assuming up till now that the agent was injected, but there's no reason it couldn't have been given orally, is there?'

I thought for a moment. 'Not in the case of digoxin, no. But with the others, tenoret and propanolol, you'd have to get the patient to swallow a hell of a lot of tablets.'

'So, not really practical?'

'I wouldn't have thought so.'

'Good,' he said, scribbling again. 'But would orally administered digoxin result in a high blood level?'

'I'm sure it would, yes.'

'I'll mention it to the lab. What about an overdose of sleeping drug — nembutal and seconol, stuff like that?'

'You could certainly use them, but they *are* controlled drugs. They're kept in a double-locked cupboard in my office.'

'OK. So potassium chloride, insulin and digoxin are the clear favourites. I'll ring Guy's now and let them know.'

When he'd finished the call, he said, 'They'll try those, but they're going to have to dilute the sample, so we probably won't get a result until tomorrow.'

I said, 'We'd better get back if we're not going to be late for Miss Shenstone.'

*

She was a small, dried-up woman with a wrinkled face — I think she was about sixty, but she looked older. Until you saw her eyes, that is. They were a bright, clear blue, and when she smiled, they took ten years from her.

She was smiling now as she stood up and reached across her desk to take Tom's hand.

'It's very good of you to see me at such short notice, Miss Shenstone,' he was saying. 'I appreciate it.'

'Not at all. I happened to have these few minutes free, and I always like to help the staff of ITU if I can.' She had a brisk, clear voice, slightly deep for a woman, with an attractive Irish lilt. 'Won't you sit down?'

'I'll leave you, then —' I began.

'I'd as soon you didn't, Sister,' Tom interrupted quickly. 'So long as you don't mind, Miss Shenstone?'

'Not at all. Now, time *is* short, so how can I help you?'

'My department is looking into ways in which costs might be cut in units such as Intensive Therapy —'

'When are they not?' Miss Shenstone inserted drily.

He smiled. 'I'm looking at several ITUs throughout the country, particularly with regard to their relation-ships with other departments, which is why I'm here.'

'We do indeed have a relationship with ITU, and a close one, but I confess I can't imagine where savings could be made . . .'

'Nor I, at this moment,' he said. 'But you'd be surprised how often, when we collate all our results, that ways of economizing do emerge.' He wasn't playing the silly ass so much, I noticed.

'I'll take your word for that,' said Miss Shenstone, glancing up at her clock.

'Perhaps I could ask you some direct questions? To save time.'

'Of course.'

He took out his notebook.

'How many operations — transplants — would you say you carried out in a week? On average.'

'It varies. Sometimes none at all, occasionally as many as five, should five suitable organs become available.'

'You say organs: do you transplant anything other than kidneys here?'

'Occasionally liver, but mostly kidney.'

'Average patient stay?'

'Anything. As little as two days in some cases, weeks in others.'

'How often would you need to use ITU, say in a week?'

'That's variable too. At the moment, we have two patients in the isolation rooms — do we not, Sister?'

I nodded. 'Yes.'

'That is more than usual — it just so happened that two of our patients required higher than usual doses of immunosuppressive drugs, which renders them more susceptible to opportunistic infections — am I losing you, Mr Jones?'

'Not at all. How long will they stay there?'

'Once again, it varies. Perhaps a week, perhaps longer.'

'What would have happened, had there been no room in ITU?'

'Then we would have approached the transplant unit in Birmingham, which is much bigger than this one.'

'I see. Do either you or ITU keep records of how often you use their facilities?'

'Indeed we do,' she said grimly. 'For purposes of cross-charging. Now that St Chad's is to become a trust.' Her tone told us what she thought about that. 'I would imagine that this is the sort of thing your department is involved in.'

He smiled without making a reply.

'I'd like to turn now to the other usage — the keeping of er . . . patients who have died on life support for purposes of transplant. I noticed earlier today —'

'Yes, I know,' she interrupted. 'But I don't think you could charge that to us. You see, it's most unlikely that any of my patients will benefit, since a match will almost certainly be found in another region and the cadaver sent there for transplant.'

'Even so, ITU facilities are being used for the benefit of transplant patients. There is a cost implication.'

'But who would be responsible for that cost, since it is not any of my patients who is the beneficiary?'

'Ultimately, I imagine the receiving hospital. But since it is your department which has instigated the usage, I think ITU should be charging you, so that it then becomes your responsibility to recover the cost from the authority in question.'

By this time, I was staring down at the floor with shame.

'But that would mean —' She broke off suddenly and I looked up to see her smile at him again. 'Mr Jones, I believe you are trying to provoke me, presumably in the hope that I will let something slip. Something to the detriment of my department. Would that be the case?'

He met her gaze. 'Why ever should I do that?'

'I don't know, Mr Jones. You tell me.'

He smiled back. 'I must apologize if I've given you the wrong impression, Miss Shenstone. I've been told that I sometimes have an unfortunate manner. What will have to be done in your case, I think, is an audit of your finances to see how best the cross-charging exercise can be implemented.'

'But wouldn't the bureaucracy involved in doing that cancel out any savings?'

'Not in the end, no. However it may seem to you,

we at the Department of Health really do try to work for the benefit of the NHS.'

'I'll have to take your word for that,' she said. She looked up at her clock again. 'However, I'm afraid that we really must bring this discussion to a close now.'

'One more question. Sister Farewell told me earlier today about your policy of organ recovery. Aren't you making a rod for your own back? In that you are doing a lot of work, not to mention incurring expense, for the benefit of other regions?'

Before she could reply, there was a knock on the door, which was then immediately opened.

'Oh, I'm sorry, Marie — I didn't realize you had company.'

'That's all right, John, just finishing. Come in.'

Dr Cannock eased his large frame into the room.

'In fact,' she continued, 'you might be interested. This is Mr Jones from the DOH. Dr Cannock, director of Pathology.'

Jones got to his feet and offered his hand, and after a fractional pause, Dr Cannock took it. He was a heavily-built, tough-looking man of about fifty with a wide, powerful face and short, grizzled hair, but with a surprisingly persuasive voice.

'Mr Jones is here looking at the relationships between ITU and other departments,' Miss Shenstone said. 'He has just asked me why we incur the work and expense of our transplant policy when it is of no direct benefit to us. I believe he thinks we should stop doing it.'

Cannock gave a laugh, creasing the flesh round his widely-spaced, dark brown eyes.

'If you would care to come along to the talk Miss Shenstone is giving tonight,' he said, 'I can assure you that not only would your questions be answered, but you would see for yourself the benefits of Miss Shenstone's policy.'

'I'd like that very much,' Jones said. 'When and where?'

'Lecture theatre at seven o'clock.'

'Thank you very much. Dr Cannock,' he continued quickly, 'I believe that your department has a relationship with ITU as well. Is there any chance I could speak to you about it sometime this afternoon? Briefly, of course.'

Cannock looked slightly taken aback. 'Well, er — I don't see why not.' He glanced at his watch. 'Three o'clock? So long as it *is* brief.'

'Thank you very much.'

'And now, Mr Jones, I really must ask you to excuse us,' said Miss Shenstone firmly.

Chapter 13

As soon as we were in the corridor, I turned on him.

'What were you thinking of,' I demanded in a low voice, 'being so rude to one of this hospital's most respected consultants?'

He manoeuvred me into an alcove and looked round before speaking.

'Do you, or do you not want this bugger found, Jo?'

'You don't have to swear at —'

'Do you?'

'Of course I do.'

'Then let me do it in my own way.'

'*Your own way* — it was certainly that! Why did you insist on having me there with you?'

'So that I could check on what she said, if necessary.'

'But she didn't say anything —'

'She might have. I'm sorry, Jo, but in this job, you

have to push if you want quick results. And in this case, we do want a quick result, before anyone else gets —'

'All right. But *has* it got you any results?'

'I don't know,' he said. 'Yet.'

I took a breath and tried to calm down. 'I'd have thought it would just put people on to you. Or put their backs up so much they'd throw you out.'

'It has been known,' he admitted with a grin. 'But then again, I've had some good breaks through what people have told me when I've wound them up. The great thing is to know just how far to go.'

I looked at him curiously. 'Yes . . . you seem to take on a different character with each person you meet.' We started walking again.

'The thing is,' I continued, 'you didn't even succeed in winding her up, did you?'

'No. I wonder why not?'

'What do you mean by that?'

He shrugged and changed the subject.

'You told me earlier that she was one of the founders of transplant surgery?'

'Yes. She carried out some pioneering research here at St Chad's in the 'sixties.'

'Then I wonder why she is still here. I mean, I don't want to be rude, but —'

'*Ha!*'

'But that unit is pretty small beer,' he finished. 'Isn't it?'

135

'Yes, I suppose it is. Latchvale's not big enough to have its own transplant unit, not with Birmingham so near, but for some reason, she didn't want to move away, so the unit stayed. Although it's subordinate to the one in Birmingham.'

As we arrived back at ITU, Viv emerged from the air-lock looking slightly flustered.

'Jo, could you come and sort out Mr Rogers?' she said. 'He thinks he's dying.'

'I'll be back in a minute,' I said to Jones as I followed her. Actually, part of me couldn't help being a little pleased; Viv did have a tendency to make one feel dispensable sometimes.

'Sister, you gotta help me,' said Mr Rogers. 'Get me a doctor, I'm having another heart attack . . .'

The other patients, those who were able, were staring on in morbid fascination.

I summoned my sunniest smile. 'No, you're not, Mr Rogers. Look —'

'But I got this terrible pain —'

'Yes, I know. Just here, I expect.' I put my hand on his chest.

'Yeah, that's right, it's —'

'You always get pain there. It's a sign that the drugs are working; that you're getting better. Look' — I pointed up at the cardiac monitor — 'that's your heart-beat. See?' I traced it with a finger. 'It's exactly as it should be. Your heart's doing fine, and so are you . . .'

Back in the air-lock, Viv said, 'I told him exactly the same things, but he wouldn't listen.'

'It could have been the other way round with a different patient,' I said, but I think we both knew that wasn't true. Viv was a good nurse, but she sometimes found it difficult to conceal her impatience with time-wasters, as she called them.

'You seem to be getting on very well with Mr Jones,' she remarked suddenly.

'How d'you mean?'

She shrugged. 'I don't know. It's almost as though you knew him before.'

'Well, I assure you I didn't.'

'I didn't think so.' She hesitated. 'He is a bit of a dickhead, isn't he?'

'Not as much as you think,' I said. 'Not when you get to know him.'

'I'll bear that in mind.'

By now, we were back at the Duty Room. He was in my office. I don't know why I'd defended him. It probably wasn't doing him any favours.

'Shouldn't you be with Dr Cannock?' I said, glancing at the clock.

'I was waiting for you.'

'Me? Why?'

'I'd assumed you were coming with me. To show me where it is, apart from anything else.'

'It's left down the corridor, then second —'

'Besides, I like having you with me, Jo.'

'I wish I could reciprocate that sentiment,' I said pointedly. I did go with him, though.

When we got to Pathology, his secretary led us past an array of spotless — almost fairground — machinery that emitted hums, buzzes and clicks and was tended by two white-coated figures, to Dr Cannock's office.

'Come in, Mr Jones. Oh, hello, Sister,' he added as he noticed me.

'Sister Farewell's helping me to compile my report,' Jones explained.

'Oh. Well, do sit down, both of you.'

We sat down.

'Now, you wanted to know about the relationship between Pathology and ITU, I believe?'

'That's right.'

'Well, I'm not sure I can be very much help to you there. As I imagine Sister has already told you, the relationship is not as cordial as it might be.'

'No, she hasn't told me that,' Jones said with a glance at me. I looked down at my hands, surprised, and a little embarrassed that Dr Cannock should have chosen to bring it up.

'Doubtless she will,' he said. 'We do, of course, perform a considerable number of laboratory tests for them.'

Jones took out his notebook. 'How many is considerable?'

He thought for a moment. 'Say, fifteen to twenty a day for ITU, although if you include the Coronary Care and Medical wards, that increases to fifty or more.'

'What kind of tests would those be?'

'Clotting tests and electrolytes on the cardiac cases. Some blood counts. Some microbiology.'

'What would they represent as a proportion of your workload?'

'Approximately a fifth.'

Jones looked up from his notebook. 'So you do a thousand tests a day here?'

'It's not so many. Like most pathology departments, we're geared for testing large numbers.'

'Yes, I noticed all the automated equipment when we were shown through.'

Cannock smiled. 'As a chemical pathologist, I've worked with automated equipment for a great many years. More recently, the problem has been in processing the large numbers of test results generated by the automation.' For the first time, his dark brown eyes gleamed with some kind of enthusiasm. 'And the answer to that problem lies in the complete computerization of the reporting system throughout the hospital.'

'I'd certainly agree with you there,' Jones commented. 'You obviously know something about computers then, Dr Cannock?'

He gave a short laugh. 'You could say that, since I'm on the working party that designed the hospital system.'

'Really? That can have been no mean task. How did you manage to fit that in with running Pathology?'

'The two aren't as incompatible as you might think. You know about the Medicines Control Agency and the Accreditation of Pathology Departments?'

'Some, yes.'

'Well, what the MCA is demanding for path labs today, they'll be demanding for hospitals tomorrow. A totally comprehensive and secure computer system. We decided to begin work on it before being ordered to.'

'I see. So what was your part in it?'

'The formulation of standard operating procedures, especially with regard to the use, and abuse, of passwords.'

Jones chuckled briefly. 'In my experience, that's virtually impossible to prevent.'

'Oh, there are ways.'

'For instance?'

'Well, if a member of staff uses the password of another who is on leave, then the system can flag this up.'

'That *is* comprehensive. And you've got that working here?'

'On a pilot basis only.' He glanced up at the clock as he spoke. 'I'm sorry, I don't want to be rude, Mr Jones, but I did say this would have to be brief, and I do have another appointment shortly.'

'Of course.' Jones closed his notebook and stood up.

'Well, thank you for giving us your time at such short notice.'

'I'm only sorry I couldn't be more help.'

'No, that was just the sort of information I was looking for.'

When we were back in the corridor, I said, 'Were you really interested in all that stuff about computers?'

'Certainly.'

'Why? It all seemed a bit creepy to me. Big Brotherish.'

'It was rather, but that could be useful to us.'

'How?'

'You'd be amazed at the amount of information you can extract from a computer, especially a nosey one.'

'I don't doubt it,' I said drily. 'But it scares me . . . it's not what hospitals and medicine ought to be about.'

'Perhaps not.' He paused. 'What did Cannock mean about the relationship between ITU and Pathology not being a cordial one?'

By now, we were back at ITU, so I said, 'I'll tell you in the office.'

Viv was on the phone in the Duty Room, which was otherwise empty.

'I was surprised he brought it up,' I said, when I'd shut the office door. 'It came about because a lot of ITUs have their own mini-labs with a lab worker to do the urgent tests. Mr Chorley wanted one here, but Dr Cannock wouldn't have it.'

'Why not?'

'He said he wanted all laboratory tests to be carried out under one roof — for purposes of quality control. He arranged for us to have exclusive use of a phlebotomist instead, so that urgent samples could be taken straight back to the lab. It still left a lot of bad feeling, though.'

'So the girl who takes the blood samples is part of Pathology?'

'Yes, either Susan or Pat are with us or in Coronary Care or the Medical ward most of the time. Usually Susan.'

'Is there really enough work to keep them busy all day?'

'In all the three wards, yes. Some patients need testing several times a day.'

He said slowly, 'What's to stop them putting something in rather than taking it out?'

'I suppose that might have been possible,' I replied after a pause, 'when we still used conventional syringes. But we don't, not any more.'

'Oh? What do you use?'

'Vacutainers. They're sample bottles that are manufactured with a vacuum in them, so they take the exact amount of blood required. There's absolutely no way anyone could use them to inject anything. I'll show you, if you like.'

I went into the Duty Room, and was looking for a set in Susan's cupboard when she came in.

'Can I help you, Sister?' she asked.

'Yes, I think you can,' I said, standing up. 'Were you about to take a sample?'

'I think so.' She picked up a couple of request forms from the tray. 'Yes.'

'Would you mind if we watched you? Mr Jones and myself?'

'Of course not.'

'Mr Jones,' I called, and he came to the door. 'Susan's about to take a blood sample, so you can see how it's done.' He stopped short. 'What, now?'

'Yes. Is that a problem?'

'No. No, not at all.'

I didn't notice how pale he was until we'd gowned up and were at the bedside. Susan set out three tubes in a rack, then screwed one end of the double-ended needle into the plastic barrel of the set. Then she applied a tourniquet to the patient's arm.

'Could you clench your fist for me please, Mr Hughes?' she said, and Mr Hughes duly obliged.

She felt his arm until she found a vein, then unsheathed the second needle of the set and quickly punctured the vein with it.

I glanced at Jones — he was deathly pale and actually trembling slightly, and a frisson of *Schadenfreude* rippled through me as I remembered something from the previous night. So the great Mr Jones had a weakness — he was needle-shy!

143

Susan took a tube from the rack and pushed it into the open end of the barrel. The rubber cap of the tube was penetrated by the needle inside the barrel and the vacuum drew in the required amount of blood. She slotted the tube in the rack and then filled the other tubes in the same way.

'Have you seen enough, Mr Jones?' I inquired sweetly.

'Yes, thank you,' he replied thickly. I thanked Susan and we left.

'You should have told me you were needle-shy,' I said as we de-gowned.

'It wasn't the needle, it was the blood,' he said, after a pause. I didn't say anything, just looked at him, and he went on, 'If you must know, my brother was a haemophiliac and the sight of blood always made me feel ill. Can we leave it at that, please?'

'Surely. I'm sorry.'

By the time we'd returned to my office, he was almost back to normal.

'Are conventional syringes ever used for blood-taking?' he asked.

'Very rarely — I can't remember the last time. Besides, a lot of patients watch when their blood's taken, and they'd notice if something were being put in with a syringe rather than taken out.'

'All right, it was just an idea,' he said after a pause. 'What other paramedics come on to the ward?'

'Jacqui, the ECG technician. The physiotherapists — they come quite a lot.' I thought. 'That's about it.'

'Would either of them ever use an invasive procedure?'

'No. Jacqui sticks on electrodes. The physiotherapist lays on hands.'

'So it comes down to a doctor or a nurse, doesn't it?' He paused. 'And of the two, a nurse has to be the more likely, wouldn't you think, Sister?'

'Would that be another example of your unfortunate manner?'

Chapter 14

I sorted out the nursing rotas for him so that he could go back to my house and study them while I looked up the action times of insulin and digoxin. For the benefit of the staff, he bade me an ostentatious goodbye, saying he would see me later at Miss Shenstone's lecture.

I left for home about half an hour after that and found him immersed in paper in my living-room.

'You look as though you could do with some coffee,' I said.

'Please. This is going to be more complicated than I'd hoped,' he continued gloomily. 'Assuming, that is, that insulin is still our favourite for the method.'

'I think it must be,' I said, 'considering its availability and ranges of times it takes to act.'

'What did you find?'

I'd discovered that soluble insulin could act in anything up to four hours, insulin zinc in anything up to six hours, and PZI in a maximum of eight to fourteen. With digoxin, the times were two hours for the injectable form and six hours for the oral.

'Let's take Mrs Sutton for example,' he said, after I'd made the coffee. 'She died at about half-past twelve in the morning. Only if she'd been given potassium chloride could it have been someone on that midnight shift.'

'That's very unlikely,' I said. 'I was on the ward myself from midnight.'

'All right. If she'd been given soluble or zinc insulin,' he continued, 'it would have been someone on the previous shift, 1600 to midnight. And if it was PZI, it could have been on the 0800 to 1600 shift.'

'More likely to have been 1600 to midnight, though.'

'More likely, yes, but not certain.'

'Unless it was in a drip as you suggested,' I said. 'Although I don't think she was on a drip . . .' I found her notes. 'No, she wasn't.'

'Just because Mrs Sutton wasn't poisoned via a drip doesn't mean that the others weren't.'

'But I thought you said yesterday that the killings were either planned or random. That would mean both.'

'If it's a psycho, as you seem to think, they might take the chance to kill whenever it occurred. Let's see how many of them were on drips when they died.'

In fact, only two out of the eight were, which is about what I'd have expected under normal circumstances.

'Which suggests to me that the killings *were* planned,' he said. 'We'll still have to consider the possibility of both, though.'

'But that'll make it impossible,' I protested.

'Tedious, perhaps, but not impossible.' He looked up. 'Why don't you make us something to eat, Jo, while I think about it?'

If, at that moment, I'd had some potassium chloride and a syringe on me, I think I might have used them. I gave him a filthy look which he didn't even notice, then went through to the kitchen and made an omelette so that I could take it out on the eggs.

He ate quickly and absent-mindedly, asking sporadic questions.

'What happens when a nurse is sick?'

'Either the shift does without, or someone else has to step in, like I did on Tuesday.'

'D'you keep records of that?'

'Yes — in that book by your elbow marked "Out of hours working".' A thought struck me. 'But wouldn't that suggest unplanned killings, just when we'd decided they're probably planned?'

'It might give the killer the opportunity they'd been waiting for, especially if it was at night. I assume there are less of you there then?'

'Less, but in an ITU, that's still a lot. That's why it's called intensive therapy.'

But sarcasm was wasted on him.

'You know what we're going to have to do, Jo?'

'I can't wait to hear.'

'We're going to have to make a chart — a list for each dead patient — of the staff who fit into the time-frame, then see which names come up on all of them.'

'I still think you'll end up with a hell of a lot of names.'

'We can worry about that later. The thing is, the accuracy of these rotas is critical. I notice in places — here for instance — that names have been crossed out and others pencilled in.'

'That's when two people have agreed to swap duties.'

'Does it have to be a swap? I mean, couldn't one simply take over the duties of another?'

'That can happen, although not often. Too tiring, for one thing. It screws up their time sheets, for another.'

'Are all such changes marked here on the rota sheet?'

'They certainly *should* be. It has been known for people to forget, although I give them hell if I find out.'

'Is there any way these rotas can be checked?'

'No, not really.'

'You mentioned time sheets just now. Do the staff fill them in themselves?'

'Yes.'

'Who signs them?'

'I do, but —'

'D'you keep copies?'

'Yes . . .'

'Well, that's how you can check these rotas.'

'But what's to stop the killer simply leaving out the times they actually killed someone?'

'The person they swapped with — they'll have put the right times.'

'But it'll take hours . . .' I protested.

'Another thing — these rotas only cover the nurses. What about the others — the doctors?'

'We keep a logbook which covers the doctors and all the paramedics.'

'We'll need that as well, then.'

'Oh, my God!'

'Beautiful omelette, Jo.'

'Oh, get lost, Jones . . .'

*

'We stand helpless in the face of the suffering and deaths of our fellow human beings. To somehow intervene in this inexorable process, however briefly, is the best expression of our humanity.'

I sat up. That had to be the most riveting start to any talk I'd ever heard, and Miss Shenstone's voice, with its dark Celtic overtones, was the best medium to convey it. Jones had left the house before me and saved me a seat near the front of the packed lecture hall.

'That statement, made by a fellow physician many years ago, is as true today as when it was first uttered.' Miss Shenstone looked around the hall. 'It was with that statement in mind that the transplant policy of this hospital was formulated.'

Dr Cannock, who as chairman of the meeting had introduced Miss Shenstone, was now sitting to one side of her on the platform, busily taking notes.

'It is our policy in this hospital to attempt to recover every single organ that becomes available, so that it may be targeted as soon as possible to the most suitable recipient, wherever they may happen to be in the country. To that end, we have a standard procedure, the first step of which is to ascertain the tissue type of every patient who is admitted to St Chad's.'

She turned, seemingly taking in every member of the audience. 'We do not want patients to die — that would defeat our purpose. But when they do, our policy is to immediately put them on life support and actively seek permission for transplant from the relatives. As soon as this is obtained, we send details of the organs available, together with the donor's tissue type, to the British Transplant Headquarters in London. They have on computer details of all the patients in the country who require transplants and can decide which of them should be the recipient. Then the donor can be sent to whichever transplant unit is to be used.' She paused again to look round.

'The successful working of this policy depends on you, ladies and gentlemen. Yes, every one of you is involved; every one of you has his, or her, part to play.'

She does have this tendency to go slightly manic sometimes when giving a talk. Not in the operating theatre, though. I remember seeing her there once when I was training, and she was utterly confident, completely in control.

'The medical and nursing staff,' she continued, 'who have the unpleasant, and at times traumatic, task of approaching the relatives of the deceased for permission for transplant. Who then place and keep the donors on life support. The medical and scientific staff who perform the tissue typing and other laboratory tests. The clerks who type the results. The porters who carry the samples. All of you.'

Having given us a large slice of the credit, she now went on to describe, with slides, case reports of recent successful transplants carried out in the unit. Not surprisingly, her audience wanted to hear about their altruism and gave her their complete attention.

When the slides were finished and the lights went up, she said, 'There has been a certain amount of . . . disquiet in the media over the last few years concerning organ transplant. The phrase *Spare Parts* has been bandied about. We have been given images of wealthy ghouls prolonging their perhaps useless lives by a form of cannibalism. Not nice at all.

'But how would you explain to a young man with a defective heart, or a young woman with failed kidneys that: Sorry, we could give you a transplant, but it's not regarded as being quite the thing?

'Transplants save lives. Young lives. Transplants very positively intervene in a human being's inexorable progress to suffering and death, which is why I make no apologies for our aggressive policy at this hospital of re-using every single available organ we can acquire. In fact, I want to see our policy extended throughout the whole country.'

There was a spontaneous burst of applause as she sat down, in which I joined, then Dr Cannock rose and asked whether there were any questions.

After the usual silence — nobody wants to be the first — a hand went up and Cannock indicated for them to speak.

'Just as a matter of interest' — the speaker was a nattily dressed man with a bow tie — 'if no suitable recipient were found in this country, could the organs be used abroad?'

Miss Shenstone said, 'That can, and occasionally does, happen, but there's nearly always a suitable recipient somewhere in this country. The usual problem is deciding which of many should receive the organs.'

Stephen, whom I hadn't noticed before, put up his hand.

'Miss Shenstone, is there not at the moment an

imbalance in the number of organs we export to other regions, compared to patients benefiting in this area? And if so, what steps could be taken to redress this imbalance?'

There was a low murmuring which might have indicated disapproval of the question, but I could appreciate his point. He was at the sharp end and, I knew, had had this question put to him.

'That's a pertinent question,' replied Miss Shenstone. 'Of course, at the moment our policy does result in an imbalance, but somebody has to lead the way. As to steps to redress this, I am at present preparing a report for the Department of Health, setting out our policy and urging that it be followed in the rest of the country. Does that answer your question?'

'Is your report likely to be acted upon?'

'I certainly hope so.'

'Thank you.'

Another hand, then I recognized Deborah Hillard's voice.

'I'd like to ask about the tissue typing of patients' samples. Are we to understand that every patient in this hospital has a sample of their blood tissue typed for the purposes of possible transplant?'

'I think I'd better answer that one myself,' said Dr Cannock with a smile. 'Nearly every patient is tissue typed, yes, and if the sole reason was for possible transplant, it would be no more . . . ghoulish than carrying a donor card. But it isn't the sole reason. Miss Shenstone and I are engaged in a piece of research at the moment trying to establish the frequency of certain rare tissue types in this country. This happens, occasionally, to coincide with Miss Shenstone's other requirements. Does that answer your question?'

'Most of it, yes. Are the patients aware that their blood is tested in this way?'

A spasm of irritation crossed Dr Cannock's face. 'Yes, in that it is covered by the consent form they sign when admitted to hospital. Dr North, I believe you had a question . . .?'

Chapter 15

When the questions had dried up, Dr Cannock thanked the sponsors, urged us to go to the reception and mini trade show they'd put up in the display hall next door, and then closed the meeting. There was a further round of applause and then the audience drifted away, some to the display hall.

'D'you want to go to the trade show?' I asked Jones.

'I certainly do.'

I shrugged and led the way through. We picked up a glass of wine and some sandwiches. 'Do you actually want to see it?'

'No, we'll just stand here for a moment.' He took a bite of sandwich. 'What did you think of it?'

'The talk? Excellent. Didn't you?'

'Oh, yes. She's an eloquent speaker.'

'Is that all you can think of to say? What about the content?'

'Oh, it seemed sincere enough, but . . .'

'But what?'

Before he could answer, we were joined by Stephen. Deborah Hillard was following in his wake.

'Hello, Jo. Mr Jones, I'm surprised to see you still here.'

'Oh? Why?'

'It *is* Friday. I'd have thought you'd have wanted to get back home.'

'Miss Shenstone suggested I come to her talk when I saw her this afternoon. I'm glad she did. It's been most interesting.'

'You enjoyed it, then?'

'Very much. As I was saying to Sister Farewell, she puts her point of view very eloquently.'

'Yes, she does. She made a very convincing case, I thought.'

'You would describe yourself, then' — this was said with a smile — 'as a disciple of hers?'

Stephen hesitated. 'I don't think I'd use the word disciple. It suggests a . . . closer relationship than exists.'

'Forgive me, Dr Wall, but I'd formed the impression that the relationship was fairly close.'

Stephen stared at him. 'What on earth makes you say that?'

'From my talk with her this afternoon, it seemed to

me that the question you put to her in the meeting was very much a question she would have wanted put.'

He smiled unwillingly. 'That is rather perceptive of you, Mr Jones. In fact, she was a contemporary of my father's at medical school and she's been a family friend ever since.' He turned to me. 'Are you feeling better now, Jo?'

'Thank you, yes. The restorative powers of sleep are remarkable.'

'I'm so glad. We were worried about you, weren't we, Debbie?'

Debbie said, 'I still think you should have gone to the police. That man Sutton is dangerous.'

'Didn't you go —?' Stephen began.

'Good evening, Dr Wall' — We looked round to see Mr Chorley — 'Dr Hillard, Sister.' He was accompanied by Miss Whittington.

'Good evening, Mr Chorley,' we chimed, almost as one. 'Miss Whittington,' I added.

'And you must be Mr Jones.' He held out a hand. 'Richard Chorley. I'm consultant in ITU.'

'How do you do, Mr Chorley.'

'Miss Whittington has told me about your visit,' Mr Chorley said. 'Are you finding it useful?'

'Very much so.'

'I must confess that I'm still somewhat in the dark as to its exact purpose.'

'We're conducting a study into the relationships

between intensive therapy units and other departments throughout the country.'

'Yes, but to what end?'

'As you must already be aware, the present government attaches great importance to the costing of every single service rendered, in order to bring costs down.'

'I imagine you're referring to cross-charging, which we've already begun.'

'I'm sure you have, but to what extent . . .?' Jones began, but at that point, we were joined by Miss Shenstone.

'Ah, Marie,' Mr Chorley greeted her. 'May I say how much I enjoyed your talk?'

She smiled. 'Of course you may, Richard.'

'That goes for all of us, I'm sure,' put in Miss Whittington.

'Thank you.'

'You've already met this young man, I understand,' said Mr Chorley, indicating Jones.

'Oh, yes, indeed. I'm so glad you could come,' Miss Shenstone said to him.

'My pleasure.'

'It seems that his masters don't feel we go far enough with our cross-charging,' Mr Chorley said to her.

'So I gather. I've already made him aware of my view — that we already go quite far enough.'

'It's not really as simple as that,' said Jones.

'Is it not?' put in Stephen, who'd been following the

conversation closely. 'Perhaps you'd like to explain why not?'

'By all means. Let's take the case of ITU and Transplant. There are two quite separate issues. Firstly, the fact that ITU is used for transplant patient recovery in some instances. That's a relatively easy cross-charging exercise, but not so the other issue, the keeping of patients on life support after death for transplants that are of benefit only to other regions.'

'That, if I may say so, is a classic example of your tunnel vision,' said Stephen. 'I refer to your department, of course, not yourself,' he added mendaciously. 'The fact is, UK patients benefit from our policy, so it must, by definition, be cost effective.'

'My view entirely,' agreed Miss Shenstone.

'I can see that there is a difference,' said Mr Chorley. 'But not an insurmountable one in terms of accountancy, I'd have thought.'

'Perhaps not,' said Jones, 'but it should nevertheless be addressed. It goes further; is there not a difference, in cost implications, between a patient who dies in ITU and is put on life support, and one who dies in another ward and is then brought to ITU for life support?'

'I must say,' said Miss Shenstone, 'I regard such distinctions not only as esoteric, but morbid and rather distasteful.'

'Hear, hear!' said Stephen.

Jones ignored him and turned to Mr Chorley. 'It's

possible that the only way to get to the bottom of it will be a full financial audit. Is any effort made to keep such figures?'

Mr Chorley regarded him thoughtfully for a moment before turning to Miss Whittington. 'Are such figures included, Ann?'

'Not as such, no, although I daresay they could be extracted from the figures we do keep.' She turned to me. 'What do you think, Sister Farewell?'

'I — er — I don't know. I expect it would be possible.'

'Morbid. Distasteful,' said Miss Shenstone.

'Mind if I join you?' It was Dr Cannock. 'What's morbid and distasteful, Marie?'

Succinctly, she told him.

'If I were you, I'd regard it as further evidence of the interest your talk has generated,' he said smoothly. 'It really has gone down extremely well. Our sponsors are very pleased with the success of their display as well. A most successful evening.'

'Thank you, John,' said Miss Shenstone. 'In no small measure due to your own efforts.'

He turned to Jones. 'Have you found it interesting, Mr Jones?'

'I certainly have,' he replied rather fulsomely. 'A most useful insight into the relationships between hospital departments.'

'If you'll excuse me,' said Mr Chorley, 'I really must go. Thanks again, Marie.'

Stephen said, 'I'll come with you if you don't mind, Mr Chorley.'

As they left, Dr Cannock said — rather maliciously, I thought — 'Insights into relationships? Would you care to give us an example of that, Mr Jones?'

'I think we've had quite enough —' Miss Shenstone began, but Jones said, 'Certainly,' and turned to Debbie, who'd been wondering whether to follow Stephen. 'Dr Hillard . . .?'

'Yes?'

'I was interested in the point you raised earlier with Dr Cannock — about blood samples being taken from patients for tissue typing tests.'

Her face showed how unwilling she was to be drawn into this. 'It was only a small ethical point.'

'But one with both interdepartmental and cost implications.'

'I wouldn't necessarily have agreed with you there,' said Dr Cannock. 'The samples are taken anyway; I simply do an extra test on them which is of benefit both to my own research, and to Miss Shenstone in those unfortunate cases in which a patient dies. Dr Hillard's point was, as she said, ethical.'

Jones turned to her. 'How so?'

Her tongue touched her lips. 'There have been cases in the last few years in which patients have sued for assault when their blood has been tested for something without their knowledge. That was my sole concern.'

'But surely,' put in Miss Shenstone, 'that's only on cases of tests for AIDS or venereal disease.'

'My point exactly,' agreed Dr Cannock. 'There can be no social stigma attached to a person's tissue type. Besides, as I indicated in my answer, permission is covered by the consent form.'

'But is there not a cost implication?' Jones persisted smoothly.

'A small one, yes, in terms of laboratory testing. But that is covered satisfactorily in my research budget.'

'Ah, yes, the research budget . . .'

'You're not intending to include that in your calculations, I hope,' said Cannock, who was clearly regretting having ever invited him to the meeting.

Miss Shenstone said firmly, 'I really think we should bring this discussion to a close. I, for one, wish to speak to the sponsors, so if you'll excuse me . . .'

'That's what I came to see you about, Marie,' said Dr Cannock. 'I'll come with you.'

'I must be going too,' said Debbie, which, after shooting Jones a poisonous look, she did.

I was expecting Miss Whittington to go as well, but she didn't.

'I must say, Mr Jones,' she said conversationally, 'I find your technique for getting information from people . . . unusual, to say the least.'

'Really, Miss Whittington? Look, can I get you some

more wine? I think there's still some left . . .' He took her glass before she had a chance to answer.

'Er — thank you . . .'

'And you, Sister Farewell.'

I silently handed him my glass and he went off.

Miss Whittington lowered her voice. 'I must say, Sister, he's not like any government official I've come across before.'

'No.'

'If I'd known he was going to be so prying, so irritating, I'd never have given permission for him to come.'

'No.'

'Perhaps I could have him withdrawn. What do you think?'

'Well — er — you couldn't do that until Monday, and —'

'That's another odd thing, isn't it? Who ever heard of a government official working over a weekend?'

'He does seem to be over-zealous, but I do have to say,' I gabbled, 'that although I agree with you about his approach, he hasn't actually caused me any problems as such yet . . .'

'You think not? Well, *I* have to say —'

She was prevented from doing this by his return.

'Thank you, Mr Jones,' she said as she took the wine glass from him.

'You're very welcome. You were saying about my technique?' he prompted.

'Yes.' She took a mouthful of wine. 'To be perfectly frank, I think some of my colleagues might not have cared for your . . . rather robust manner of questioning them.'

'Oh dear. I have been told I sometimes have an unfortunate manner. The trouble is, Miss Whittington,' he confided, 'that we in the DOH sometimes feel that we can't win. We're accused of being out of touch with the real world, but when we make an honest attempt to get in touch with it, we're accused of interference, or worse.' He looked quite hurt.

She smiled tightly. 'That may be so, Mr Jones, but I think you know perfectly well what I mean.'

'Miss Whittington, you have my assurance that I will try to be more . . . circumspect for the rest of my visit.'

'How long *are* you intending to stay with us?'

'I can't be sure exactly,' he said cheerfully. 'I'll let you know as soon as I can.'

'Please do. And I hope you will be more circumspect.'

'You have my assurance on that.'

'So you said.' She drained her glass. 'I think I'll bid you both good night.'

'She's not as daft as she appears,' he said, as soon as she was out of earshot.

'Which is more than can be said for you,' I hissed furiously. 'A lot of people are going to be wondering about you after this evening's performance — one minute playing the silly ass, then flashes of perception, then trying to shock people by being rude to them. You know Miss Whittington wanted to give you your marching orders, don't you?'

'But she didn't, did she?'

'Only because I intervened on your behalf — told her you weren't a problem to me — may God forgive me for such a lie.' I took a breath. 'There isn't a single person here you haven't offended in some way or another tonight. Why? If any of these people are involved, which I very much doubt, they'll be on to you by now. Is that what you wanted?'

'You're raising your voice. Calm down.'

I looked around. The crowd was thinning, but Dr Cannock was still there, talking with the sponsors. Standing a little apart were Stephen and Miss Shenstone. She shot us a glance as Stephen said something to her.

I said, calmly, 'I simply can't understand you.'

He said, 'We'll talk about it when we get back to your house, shall we?'

'Oh. You do feel ready to go, then?'

'Yes, I think so.'

I tried to swallow my irritation. 'Do we need to stagger our departures?'

'I suppose we'd better. Give me a minute or two, then follow.' He handed me his wine glass and turned to go.

I slowly took the glasses back to a table. There were

few people left now and I was on the point of leaving myself when I saw Stephen walking rapidly towards me.

'Jo, wait . . .'

I couldn't really ignore him without it looking odd. 'Yes?'

'I was trying to ask you earlier . . . what did happen about the man who threatened you?'

'Oh, it was nothing, like you said. A storm in a teacup.' I started walking towards the door.

'So he didn't bother you any more?' He walked beside me.

'No.'

'I'm glad about that. It's just that I don't seem to have had a chance to speak to you lately.'

Ha!

'We've all been busy.' I kept walking.

'Yes. That chap Jones who was with you, has he gone?'

'Yes.'

'Seems an odd sort of cove.' It was said casually, but when I looked at him, he was studying my face.

'I suppose he is, rather.'

'Jo, I was wondering . . .'

'If you don't mind, Stephen, I'd really like to go home. I'm exhausted.'

'OK, Jo . . .' He fell behind me.

As I walked to my car, I wondered whether I'd done

the right thing . . . perhaps if I'd allowed myself to be persuaded a little more . . .

No.

To my surprise, Jones was waiting for me in his car. He raised a hand when he saw me and started driving off.

I got into my own car and followed him out. Wiped the screen with my hand and switched on the demisters, hoping they'd warm up soon.

No, Stephen would have to show a lot more contrition; work a lot harder than that before . . .

The road from the hospital rises gently for about a quarter of a mile and then dips again just before the junction with the main road.

Jones stopped as the lights changed and I pulled up behind him. At least, I would have done, had my brakes been working. I pumped the pedal frantically, then remembered the hand brake — too late, though, to prevent my car from ploughing, in slow motion, into the back of the Cooper.

Chapter 16

The shunt pushed his car, also in slow motion, about five yards into the traffic pulling away from the lights. Cars braked, swerved, hooted.

He jumped out, ran back and yanked open my door.

'What the hell are you playing at, Jo?'

'My brakes failed,' I said numbly.

'All right,' he said after a moment. 'We'll have to move the cars. Can you move yours?' His voice came from far away. 'Are you all right?'

'I don't know.'

'Better let me do it.'

I extricated myself from the seat, my body not belonging to me. He started the engine and drew back on to the grass verge, then jumped out to move his own car behind it. Then he guided me into the passenger seat.

'Better?'

'No.' I drew heavily on a cigarette I couldn't remember lighting.

'Can you tell me what happened?'

'*Nothing* bloody happened, that was the trouble.'

'No response to the brakes at all?'

'No.'

He reached across me, opened the glove compartment and took out a torch.

'Wait here; I won't be long.'

Where did he think I was going? I wondered, and began to shiver, just a little at first, then violently.

He came back. 'Somebody's cut through the brake pipes,' he said.

'Who?' My lips framed the word.

'Sutton,' he said in a low voice. 'It's time he was put to rights.'

'Now?'

'Oh, yes.' Then, noticing for the first time the tremor in my voice: 'Are you cold?'

'I'm bloody terrified.'

He opened the glove compartment again. 'You won't be doing any more driving tonight, so have some of this.' He handed me a small flask. 'Not too much. I'm going to check my lights.'

It was whisky. I took a hefty swallow, then another. Heard him tinkering at the back of the car. Felt slightly better.

He reappeared with a screwdriver, took one of the back lights off my car and disappeared again. More tinkering.

'Any better?' he said, climbing back in.

'A bit. Thanks.'

'I had to take one of your lights, in case you hadn't noticed.'

I didn't reply.

He started the engine and backed on to the road. Without thinking, I reached for the seat belt.

'Where are we going?' I asked when I realized it wasn't to my house.

'Sutton.'

Panic gripped me. 'We can't! He'll kill us . . .'

'No, he won't.'

'Why can't we go to the police?'

'Because I can do this better,' he said, and I realized he was in a cold fury.

'Not me. Stop the car!' It came out as a squeak.

'When we get there. I'll need your help, Jo.'

I looked at him, appalled.

'What are you going to do?'

'Like I said, put him to rights.' He glanced at me. 'Don't worry. He won't do anything.'

Less than a minute later, we pulled up in a quiet avenue and I dimly wondered how he knew the address.

'Listen, Jo — we go up to the door. It's bound to

have a spy hole. You ring, I stand to one side. When it opens, say you want to speak to Sutton. OK?'

'No, I —'

But he'd already opened his door and was helping/pulling me out from the other side.

We walked quickly up the gravelled drive. As we approached the porch, a blinding light came on.

'It's automatic — keep going.'

We reached the porch. I was trembling violently again. He left me in front of the door, and standing to one side, pressed the button on the intercom, leaving his finger on it.

The rattle of the spy hole flap, then a metallic voice on the intercom, 'Aw right, aw right . . .' Polo's voice. 'Whadda you want?'

'I want to speak to Sutton.'

'Oh, it's you.' He laughed. '*Mr* Sutton to you, honey.' The bolts drew back . . . my throat closed as the door opened . . .

'Aw right, you'd better co —'

'Back! Now!' Jones was in the doorway, gun pointed at his belly. Polo hesitated and backed off. I followed him in.

'Close the door, Jo.'

'I could get really irritated with you, mister,' Polo said softly.

'Hands behind your head.'

Again, slowly, he obeyed.

'Who is it, Polo?' Sutton's voice, coming nearer. Polo looked to say something, but Jones levelled the gun.

Sutton appeared. Somehow, I had the time to notice how drawn he looked. His eyes flicked from Jones to me. 'Is this him, Polo?'

'Yes, boss. Sorry.'

'What d'you want?' he said to Jones. He didn't look worried, just tired. His casual clothes were good quality, yet he somehow looked untidy.

'You fixed the brakes on Miss Farewell's car. Do anything, *anything*, like that again and I'll fix you.'

'Not me,' he said. 'I didn't fix her brakes. But *you*' — he pointed at him — 'are a dead man.'

Jones smiled and shook his head. 'Not me, Sutton. I'm a friend of Major Hatherleigh's. Remember him? Hereford's not a million miles from here.'

Silence, then, 'He know you're here?'

Jones nodded. Sutton drew a breath.

'We'd better talk, then. There's no need for that.' He waved at the gun and Jones lowered it. '*No*, Polo!'

Polo had started forwards, but Sutton's voice stopped him. 'Not a finger. Right? You'd better come through,' he said to us.

The house was very warm, I noticed, the carpets very thick. He led us down a hall and into a large living-room, indicated a leather sofa. We both sat on the edge. Everything was bright colours and money, and yet, in a strange way, it had a style. Sutton went over to a sideboard.

'I had nothing to do with that robbery at his sister's place,' he said. 'Drink?'

'Whisky,' said Jones. No nonsense about ladies first, I noticed. 'Unfortunately for you, he thinks you did. So do I.'

'Sister?'

I realized he was talking to me. 'Oh, I'll have a whisky too, please.'

He brought the drinks over.

'The villains that did it are banged up; what more's he want?'

'The man behind it.'

Sutton looked at me. 'I didn't fix your car, Sister. Why should I?'

'As a frightener,' said Jones. 'A warning.'

'Tell me what happened.'

'You know what happened.'

'Tell me.'

I said, 'My brakes failed at the junction of Manor Road and Tolworth Road and I rammed the back of Mr Jones's car.'

'Traffic lights near the hospital?'

'Yes.'

'So if he hadn't been in front, you could've been killed?'

'Yes.'

'Why should I want to kill you, Sister? If I wanted to frighten you, I'd frighten you, not risk killing you.'

'It was a calculated risk,' Jones said. 'You thought she'd probably realize the brakes weren't working before anything —'

'I buried my wife this morning,' Sutton interrupted. 'The sister says someone killed her. I want that bastard. I'm not likely to get him with her dead, am I?'

Jones hesitated. 'I still say you were trying to —'

'Oh, for Chrissake! If someone fixed her brakes, it was probably the bastard we're after.'

In a flash, I believed him. Jones had pushed someone too far.

'Then why didn't they do my car as well?'

'How long have you been up here?'

'Since yesterday.'

Was that all? I wondered.

'Then he don't know which your car is, does he, you berk?'

'You can cut that out.'

'Well?'

'I need to think about it.' It was the first time I'd heard Jones on the defensive.

'You do that.' He finished his drink. 'An' not in my house.'

'I'm not through yet.'

Sutton just looked at him.

'I'll find the person behind these killings, then I'll

hand them over to the law. I'm sorry about your wife, but it's for the law to handle, not you.' He finished his drink. 'Thanks for the whisky.' He stood up. 'We'll see ourselves out.'

Sutton didn't move, just said quietly, 'Don't push me too far.'

My legs were still shaking, or had they started again? In the hall, Polo said, 'I'll remember you, mister,' as he opened the door.

'So you keep saying.'

In the car, I said in a shaking voice, 'I told you after the mortuary not to do anything like that to me again,' then burst into tears.

He held me, rocked me. 'I'm sorry, Jo, but it was worth it.'

I hated him for that, but there was nowhere else I could turn for comfort. After a while, I said, 'Can we go back home, please?'

I smoked as he drove back through the town, thinking, is this really the place where I grew up?

I said, 'What about my car?'

'Tell the police about it when we get in. Tell them you'll shift it tomorrow.'

After another pause, I said, 'They know, don't they? Whoever's doing this — they know about you.'

'Looks like it.'

'What's to stop them trying again?'

'Me.'

'You didn't stop them fixing — is that the word? — my brakes!' I shouted.

He didn't reply and a few minutes later, he stopped outside my house. I got out, slammed the door and found my housekey. He joined me as I was inserting it.

I said suddenly, 'How do we know there isn't somebody in there now?'

He knelt and took something from the bottom of the door.

'There's nobody in there.' He took the key from me and opened it. 'See?'

I followed him inside.

'What did you do?'

'Stuck a piece of Sellotape across the crack whenever we left.' He held it up. 'Still intact. No one inside.'

I had to smile. 'You took a hell of a risk with Sutton though, didn't you?'

'Not really. I knew he wouldn't do anything once I mentioned Hatherleigh.'

'Who is Hatherleigh?'

'A major in the SAS. Sutton didn't know that when he set up the robbery at his sister's house.'

'What happened?'

'She was pregnant at the time and the shock nearly lost her the baby. If she had have, Sutton would be dead by now. As it was, the villains were caught, but nothing could be proved against Sutton. Hatherleigh found out though, and . . . communicated with him to the effect that it would take very little to persuade him to kill him. Sutton believed him. Still does.'

'Evidently. And you're a friend of this Major Hatherleigh? Were you in the SAS?'

He laughed out loud. 'No, and no. I was in the army for three years, before my time in the police, but nothing like that. I have — let's say a contact, who told me all this.'

'Would that be the Andy who rang just after you arrived?'

The smile left his face. 'I'd prefer you forgot that name. Why don't you make us some coffee?'

It was on the tip of my tongue to tell him to make his own damned coffee, but he was being unusually forthcoming and I wanted him to go on talking.

'Tom, who cut my brakes?'

'The person we're after.' He followed me into the kitchen.

'How did they know?' I filled the kettle.

'They must have picked it up sometime today.'

'At the meeting?'

'Perhaps,' he said slowly. 'I wouldn't have thought they'd have had enough time, though. Who knows your car?'

'Stephen, obviously. Maybe Debbie Hillard, maybe Miss Whittington.'

'Did you notice Wall talking to Miss Shenstone just before we left?'

'Yes. But if they know each other, so what? And I know Stephen. He may be a shit, but he's not a killer.'

He thought about that for a moment. 'How long have you known him?'

I spooned coffee into mugs. 'About three months, I suppose.'

'I mean, intimately.'

'Two weeks,' I said reluctantly. 'Three.' The kettle boiled and we took our coffees back to the living-room.

'Tom, why were you so offensive to all those people?'

'Provocative — not the same thing. Because it makes people react. As I told you earlier, I've found it very useful in the past.'

'Well, they certainly reacted tonight, didn't they?' I said bitterly.

'I've said sorry. Haven't I?'

'Not that I remember.'

'I'm sorry.'

'Did you see any other reactions?'

He made a face. 'Not that add up at the moment.'

'If it wasn't for the fact of my brakes,' I said, 'I couldn't believe it was any of those people. Not *those* people. It's someone lower down. A psychopath.'

He sighed. 'You could be right. But I just can't get it out of my mind that seven of those eight victims had their organs transplanted.'

'But that would have to mean Miss Shenstone, and I can't believe that. Nor could I believe Mr Chorley.'

'Whoever it is, we'll start eliminating them tomorrow. There's no reason why you shouldn't go in tomorrow, is there? Researching for facts?'

'No. Except that one person'll know why.'

'They do already. Jo,' he looked up, 'you haven't phoned the police about your car yet, have you? Better do it now.'

They already knew it was there and asked how long it would be before I removed it. I told them I hoped tomorrow. They told me they hoped so too. I stuck my tongue out at the receiver before putting it down.

'They told you by tomorrow,' Tom said from the sofa.

'That's right.' I glanced at the clock. It was nearly eleven, late enough, but I felt as though it should be later.

'I'm going to bed,' I said.

'Fine. See you tomorrow.'

I used the bathroom and climbed into bed. But not to sleep.

Although I was so tired, as soon as I closed my eyes, I found myself re-living that split second when I realized my brakes weren't working . . .

Shouldn't have had the coffee. Tried reading for a while, but I was so tired that I couldn't concentrate, and yet I still couldn't sleep.

I heard him come up to the bathroom. As he came out, I called his name.

'Yes?' He was outside my door.

'I can't sleep. I'm scared.'

He came in and sat on the bed.

'I'm sorry about today,' he said awkwardly. 'About my methods. Your brakes. That won't happen again, I promise you.'

'I keep going over it . . . if you hadn't been in front . . . Tom, please hold me.'

He hesitated, then kicked off his shoes.

'It'll be all right, I promise.' He put his arms around me.

It was so warm. He was so compact. I found his mouth, kissed him. He responded, then drew away.

'Don't think I don't want to,' he said in a low voice. 'But it wouldn't help us. Not now.'

To my relief, he didn't go, just lay beside me, holding me until I went to sleep.

Chapter 17

I slept late, which probably didn't do me any harm, and came down to find Tom in the kitchen.

'I've made a mess of pottage,' he said. 'Want some?'

'I've no birthright to offer.'

'Well, actually, it's porridge. Still a mess, though. You can have some for nothing, if you like.'

'You forget how nice it is,' I said, a few minutes later. 'What's the plan for today?'

'First, phone the garage about your car, and then I'll run you into the hospital.'

'Why? Oh, the nursing rotas.'

'Yes. Check them as best you can, then see if you can put together a timetable for the doctors and paramedics for the last couple of months.'

'As I said yesterday, it'll take me a while. What will you do?'

'Oh, there were a couple of things I wanted to check out,' he said noncommittally. 'Which reminds me: the lab tests. I'll try Guy's now.'

I made some coffee while he went to the phone.

'Really?' I heard him say. 'That *is* good news . . . yes . . . thanks.'

'Well?' I said as he came back into the kitchen.

'Eureka!' he said softly, grinning.

'Well, *what*?'

'Insulin. At least four times the amount needed to kill her.'

'Did they say what type?'

'They haven't done that yet. But it's the evidence that you were right all along, Jo.'

*

He dropped me a little way outside the hospital gate. The first person I saw when I arrived at the ward was Emma.

'Hello, Jo,' she said. 'I'd have thought you'd seen enough of this place during the week.'

'I'm getting some figures together for Mr Jones.'

'Oh. Couldn't that have waited until Monday?'

'Apparently, he needs them for Monday. Everything OK here?'

'Fine. Viv's in the clean area. Oh — Mr Phillips died last night.'

'I see. Not entirely unexpected, although I had hoped . . .'

'Yes.'

It was rather ironic. Mr Phillips, of the wandering hands had, against the odds, improved and been moved to Coronary Care. Then he'd relapsed and returned to us, and now he was dead. I shivered. From the moment he'd first come in, I'd not thought his chances good . . .

I started on the rota. Although it was a long, boring job, the fact that I'd now been vindicated somehow made it less painful. Debbie Hillard came in and asked me what I was doing. Helping Mr Jones to collect figures, I replied.

'Oh, he's still around, is he?' she said darkly. 'I've got a bone to pick with him. Where is he?'

'Not here yet. He said he'd look in sometime during the morning.'

She grunted and stalked out.

A little while later, Viv came in.

'Ain'tcha got no 'ome to go to?'

I told her I was helping Mr Jones with his figures.

'Oh, him. Well, so long as he's not helping you with yours.'

She peered over my shoulder. 'What you doing, then?'

I thought quickly. 'Oh, he wants to know whether the time sheets correlate with the rotas, for some reason.'

'Nosey bugger, in't he?'

'Yes, he is, rather.'

She went out.

When I'd finished that, I found the Duty Room logbook and began making a timetable from it of the doctors and paramedics. This wasn't quite so painful, since there weren't anything like so many of them.

Tom managed to time his entrance shortly before I'd finished.

'Did you find what you were looking for?' I asked in an undertone, still curious to know what it was.

'Thank you, yes. How about you?'

'Nearly there.'

He waited while I finished, then I ceremoniously handed the sheets over to him and he left. Debbie glared after him but didn't attempt any bone-picking. I hung around a little longer, then phoned for a taxi.

He'd already started setting up his chart on the table in the living-room when I got home.

'Wouldn't it be easier if you got a computer to work that out for you?' I asked.

'Mm? Oh yes, certainly.' He sat up. 'As a matter of fact, there is one. It's called HOLMES.'

'As in Sherlock?'

'That's right.' He grinned. 'Actually, it's an acronym. Home Office Large Major Inquiry System.'

'Why not use that?'

'It would take too long to set up — it's a main frame system and we'd have to go to Birmingham.' He sighed. 'Although looking at this lot, it might come to that.'

'I wonder there isn't a micro version.'

'I've wondered that, too. Probably because no micro computer would be big enough to handle the software. It's vast.'

He returned to his chart, so I took the opportunity to do some housework and washing.

We took a short break an hour or so later for some lunch, then he went back to it.

An hour after that, he threw down his pencil. 'Well, I've narrowed it down to ten people so far as availability goes.'

I looked up from the book I'd been reading. 'Who are they?'

He read them out. 'Mary Tamworth. Stephen Wall. Sophie Marsh. Vivien Aldridge. Josephine Farewell —'

'Oh, thank you very much!'

'It's what HOLMES would have come up with. Emma Riley. Susan King. James Croxall. Helen Armitage. And Paul Ridware.'

'Well, none of them exactly leap out at you, do they?' I observed. 'It sounds to me as though you will have to ask HOLMES. Surely eight deaths counts as both large and major.'

'I suppose so.' He looked round. 'Where did the patient record printouts go?'

'Over here.' I handed them to him. 'Fancy a coffee?'

He gave a grunt which I took to be affirmative.

I'd just brought the coffee out when the phone went. It was my mother, wondering why they hadn't seen me for over a week. I explained that I'd been busy and would come as soon as I could.

'Why not come over for tea this afternoon, dear?' she asked.

'I can't, I'm sorry —'

'There's something odd here,' Tom said.

'Have you got someone with you, dear?'

'Yes, I have.'

'Well, bring him too. We don't mind.'

'He's here on business,' I said quickly. Mum would like nothing more than to see me married off.

'I think this is it,' Tom said, the excitement mounting in his voice.

'*What*?'

'Are you still there, dear?'

'Mum, something important's happened. I'll phone you back. Love to Dad.' I slammed down the receiver and went over to him. 'What is it?'

He was holding the patient records. 'D'you realize?' he began, but before he could get any further, the doorbell rang . . . 'Don't let them in,' he murmured. I went over and opened the door against the chain.

'Hello, Jo.'

'Stephen!'

'I'm sorry I missed you this morning . . .'

'Pardon?'

'I wanted to speak to you, but I missed you this

morning, when you were in. I just wanted to make sure you were all right.'

'Well, I am, thank you.'

'Can I come in for a moment?'

'Er — well, it's rather an awkward time . . .' I began, then inspiration struck . . . 'I was just on my way to see my parents.'

'I won't keep you long,' he persisted.

'Well, it really is awkward,' I said firmly. 'I've left the bath running. I'll ring you.'

'All right,' he said after a pause.

'Thanks for calling, anyway,' I said, and shut the door. And at that moment, I realized he was out of my system — I didn't want to see him again no matter what he did.

'Has he gone?' Tom asked quietly.

'Yes.'

'I wonder what he wanted,' he mused, half to himself.

'Guilty conscience, I expect,' I said. 'Never mind him, what have you found?'

'Mm? Oh yes, the patient records. D'you realize that seven out of the eight victims are marked down under religion as either: *None, Agnostic or Atheist?*'

Once again, I felt an acute sense of disappointment. 'So what? We get quite a few these days who say *None*, at least.'

'Three of these are *Atheist*, two each for *Agnostic* and *None*. How often do people going into hospital, especially an ITU, claim they're atheist?'

'It does happen.'

'Seven out of eight times? Come on, that can't be coincidence.'

'Then why not eight out of eight? Who is the eighth?'

'Mrs Sutton. A gangster's wife who tried to commit suicide, which is one of the great religious taboos. Jo, how many patients, say out of ten, claim to be any of those things?'

'I don't know —'

'Then let's go in and look.'

'No, let me think a minute.' I shut my eyes, trying to visualize the records. 'I'd say two or three, although it's only a guess.'

'Out of ten. A bit different from seven out of eight. So which of our ten suspects, sorry, nine, are religious freaks?'

'I can only think of two,' I said slowly, unwillingly.

'Well?'

'Emma Riley, and Susan King.'

'Emma Riley . . .' His eyes flickered away from me, back again. 'Isn't she that really . . . attractive one?'

'Yes, and she's more than just attractive, as I'm sure you've noticed. She's also old-fashioned, goes to church, and a bit of a prude.'

'Boyfriends?'

'I think so. But she doesn't talk about them.'

'Does she . . . flaunt her religiosity?'

'How d'you mean?'

'Does she go on about it? Make a thing of it.'

'No. She's just self-contained.'

'All right, what about the other one, Susan King? Rather plain, as I remember.'

'Yes. She doesn't flaunt her religiousness either, but I know she belongs to one of those weird sects that think everything's a sin. She's always going away on courses and retreats with them.'

'Sounds more likely, doesn't it? And you were sure yourself that it was an individual, a psycho . . .'

'Tom, she's a phlebotomist. I showed you yesterday how it would be impossible for her to inject anything into a patient.'

'Because all blood samples are taken with that vacuum thing?'

'That's right. Vacutainer.'

'Can I use your phone?'

'Go ahead.'

He keyed in a number and waited.

'Holly? It's Tom . . . yes, I'm fine thanks, love. How about you?'

His wife, obviously. I turned away, feeling a totally unjustified spurt of jealousy. I still listened, though.

'Holly, have you ever used vacutainers? . . . Yes . . .' Silence while he listened . . . 'I see . . . Look, suppose you took one of those containers and used a syringe to squirt in some liquid, and then pumped in some air after it?' Another pause . . . 'Ahhh, I thought so . . .

Yes, you've been a great help . . . I've got to go now. I'll ring you later, bye.'

He looked up at me.

I said, 'Explain it again, please.'

'You've got the double-ended needle screwed into the barrel, right?'

'Yes?'

'You stick the outside needle into a vein, then press the tube with its vacuum into the barrel, so that the inside needle penetrates the rubber bung of the tube and the vacuum sucks in the blood.'

'Oh . . .' I said, understanding.

'Yes. If you put a pressure into the tube instead of a vacuum, it will inject whatever liquid you may have put into it.'

'And it would be easy enough to use a conventional syringe and needle to do that,' I said slowly. 'To put insulin into the tube instead of anti-coagulant, and then pressurize it with air.'

'Exactly.'

'Yes, I think you're right. I remember now how the deaths stopped when Susan went on leave for two weeks, and then Mrs Sutton died the day after she came back. But the timing . . .? Mrs Sutton died at about half-past twelve in the morning.'

'What time does Susan leave in the afternoon?'

'Around five, usually.'

'An hour later than the nursing shift. And five until

twelve is only seven hours, which is within your time range for PZI. Would she be able to get hold of it?'

'Yes, I'm afraid she would.' I looked up. 'But what about the brakes on my car? How did she know we were looking for a killer?'

He drummed with his fingers on the table top. 'I've got it. Remember when your printer went down — the fuse? The patient record came out in the Duty Room, and she was in there. She'd have seen it.'

'Especially as Viv brought everyone's attention to it. But would that have been enough for her to —?'

'Yes, I think it would. It was the first victim, or at least, the first one you spotted. He died nearly two months ago. Why print that out now? And especially just after a Man from the Department has arrived.'

'But how did she know where my car would be?'

Again, he thought.

'Yesterday afternoon. I left at about four — remember? And told you in a loud clear voice that I'd see you at Miss Shenstone's lecture.'

'All right, you've convinced me,' I said. 'But what are we going to do? We've got to stop her before she kills anyone else.'

'We have to go to the police, obviously. Which means coming clean about the mortuary.' He picked up the phone again.

'Marcus?' His boss. 'It's Tom. I think we've found our killer, but there's a problem . . .' He told him what had happened and asked him to clear the mortuary break-in with the police.

*

An hour later, we were with a rather irritated Inspector Anslow.

'I wish you'd told us earlier you were here, Mr Jones.'

'Would you have taken it seriously? In the circumstances?'

'Perhaps,' he said, although I didn't believe him. 'You could at least have told us about the break-in to the mortuary.'

'Well, I'm telling you now, aren't I?' Another example of the unfortunate manner, I supposed.

'Yeah, after we've already spent umpteen man hours on it.' He sighed. 'All right, Mr Jones, you've persuaded me, but there's nothing like enough evidence for a conviction on what we've got.' He paused. 'I suppose she might break down under interrogation . . . what do you think, Miss Farewell?'

'I wouldn't bank on it,' I said, thinking of Susan's set and determined expression.

'So what do we do?'

'We could set a trap,' said Tom. 'We could set it up tomorrow and spring it on Monday.'

Anslow looked at him suspiciously. 'What kind of a trap?'

Tom told him.

Chapter 18

Monday morning. The trap was set. We waited.

It's the hardest part, the waiting; at least, so runs the cliché, but as is so often the case, the cliché's right. That's why they become clichés, I supposed . . . My mind tumbled with thoughts and suppositions, most of them as irrelevant as that.

It seemed incredible that the plan could have been set up so quickly. Mr Chorley had had to be told of course; also, Miss Whittington. She'd been deeply shocked and had not wanted to be directly involved. But Mr Chorley was made of different stuff, and as he conducted the ward round that morning, there was no perceptible change in his demeanour.

Oh, and James. He had to be told as well. No one else knew.

As morning became afternoon, the final piece was put into place. We waited . . .

*

The police had wanted to wait a few days before setting the trap, to lull any suspicions Susan might have had, but Mr Chorley wouldn't countenance it.

'Who knows whom she will take it into her head to kill next?' he'd demanded. 'We simply can't afford to take that risk. She *must* be arrested tomorrow . . .'

And Mr Chorley had friends in high places, so the trap was set . . .

That Sunday evening, we'd been driving back from the police station. There was a rich autumn sunset and the Ladies of the Vale stood out black against it.

'I've never seen a cathedral with three spires before,' Tom said, breaking the silence.

'The Ladies of the Vale.'

'Beg your pardon?'

I repeated it. 'That's what they're called.'

He looked in his mirror and indicated to the right. 'Let's have a closer look.'

I glanced at him. 'Are you a religious freak, too?'

He laughed. 'No. I do like old churches and cathedrals, though. They're a link with the past. They . . . they define a town somehow.'

'Take the next left.'

A few minutes later, he pulled up under the west front.

'It's strange,' I said, looking up at the rows of saints and holy men, 'I've never really thought much about this building, until recently.'

'What brought it on?'

'I don't know. I've just had this feeling of the spires, the Ladies, keeping watch over the city, brooding over the centuries.'

He smiled. 'You're a romantic. Shall we have a look inside?'

'It's Sunday — there might be a service or something,' I protested. 'After all, it is what they're there for.' He'd already opened his door, though. I followed him. A trio of pigeons clattered away.

The huge wooden doors in the middle of the front were obviously bolted shut. He found a smaller door to one side which he pushed open. We heard singing.

'There is a service,' I said.

'We can still have a quick look.'

Rather reluctantly, I followed him in. The purity of the choral voices shimmered around the stone columns and arches and up into the vault. There was a congregation of perhaps three or four dozen. Brasswork gleamed dully in the stained light. The organ trembled.

'Tom, let's go,' I whispered.

'Why?' He smiled. 'Are you about to turn into dust or something?'

'I just don't feel comfortable.'

He shrugged and we went out. He said, 'I thought it was rather lovely.'

'Oh, it was; it was beautiful. But we were intruding.'

Back in the car, I said, 'What a strange place for us to be. Considering the . . . perversity of what we've been doing.'

He was staring up at the spires. 'Ladies of the Vale,' he mused. 'Well, there's been you, Susan . . .'

'Oh, thanks!'

'So who's the third?'

'Miss Whittington?' I said, catching his mood.

'No . . .'

'Miss Shenstone, then? But as I said in the beginning, she's a near saint.'

'I don't believe in saints,' he said, thoughtfully. 'People do what they do because they want to.' He looked around warily. 'Although perhaps this isn't the best of places to say so.'

He started the car and we got home without being struck by any thunderbolts. I made a meal. He had still been very thoughtful, for some reason . . .

*

Monday, twelve-fifteen. Susan came into the Duty Room, picked up the pathology request forms from the basket and looked through them before going to the cupboard to replenish her tray.

Helen Armitage asked Mary some fool question and

got a dusty answer. Gail came in complaining: 'That Mr Bridges, he's the limit . . .'

'Why, what's he done now?'

'Oh, it's the way he turns everything you say into a sexual innuendo . . .'

All their voices were unreal.

Quietly, unobtrusively, Susan picked up her tray and went out.

*

Earlier that morning, James had come into the Duty Room just after Susan.

'No boyfriend today then, Jo? I thought something was missing.'

'If it's Mr Jones you're referring to, he went home on Saturday,' I said in a bored voice.

'And good riddance,' muttered Debbie Hillard from the corner.

'Why?' James demanded. 'I didn't think he was that bad.'

'I don't suppose he dropped you in it the way he did me.'

But would Susan take the bait so soon after Tom's departure . . .?

*

It had been decided that I shouldn't be on the ward when Susan went in, in case my presence put her off, so I got the story from James later.

He was sitting with Mr Dunn at the time, an RTA who'd apparently been drunk when he'd crashed his car. Susan came in, glanced at her forms and approached a bed.

'Mr Bridges?' she said softly.

'That's right,' said Gail, an edge to her voice.

Susan set out the sample bottles and punctured Bridges's vein ('Ooh, that's a nasty prick you got there, miss.' Gail rolled her eyes).

Next came Mrs West, then Mr Dunn . . .

'Am I in your way, love?' asked James.

'If you wouldn't mind, just for a minute.' Her quiet voice was as assured as ever.

'The lady's going to take a sample of your blood,' James said to Dunn, then eased his way past her. Dunn mumbled something unintelligible. His head was so heavily bandaged that only his eyes were visible, and one arm was encased in plaster.

James wandered over to the nurses' station, said something to Armitage, then wandered back as Susan was setting out her sample bottles. He watched her for a moment, then nodded once in Dunn's direction. She put a bottle in the barrel of the vacutainer assembly. As she went to puncture Dunn's arm, his hand appeared from beneath the bedclothes (the plaster was a blind) and fastened on to her wrist . . .

'Susan King, I am arresting you for attempted —'

In a flash, she twisted her hand away and rammed

the needle into his biceps . . . he roared and tried to pull it out . . .

James went to grab her, but she picked up her tray and flung it at him, its edge catching his forehead before crashing on to the floor, then she bolted for the left-hand patient transfer air-lock, where she propped the outer door open (so that the inner door was locked).

The policeman outside had been fooled by her plain appearance and had a knee in the groin and fingernails in his eyes before he knew it, and by the time Anslow and Co had reached him, she'd completely disappeared.

Anslow quickly organized the hunt before venting his spleen on the unfortunate Dunn (his real name) and his colleague outside (whose eyes were still watering).

The hospital was painstakingly searched and road blocks set up before someone thought to tell him that Susan always travelled by push-bike. Her flat was broken into, but there was no sign of her.

Then, two hours after she escaped, it was reported that someone answering her description had boarded a Birmingham train with a bicycle. The headquarters of her religious sect — Disciples of the One True God — was based in Birmingham, so the search was concentrated there.

'At least her guilt's beyond doubt now,' Tom said to me. 'I was worried that she'd just flatly deny everything.

Even with this' — he indicated the pressurized bottle of insulin in its plastic bag — 'they might have had a job convicting her.'

Dunn had been admitted the evening before with the word *Atheist* firmly planted in his record (Tom had discovered that Susan looked through the new patient records on the computer every day, using the password of one of the lab workers). The word had been put round that he had been driving while drunk and that a child had been killed in the accident.

Tom had been reported to have left at last and a request for blood samples from Dunn put into the basket at midday. James had sat with him until Susan appeared. After moving away, he'd waited until he'd seen her take a bottle from her pocket, then nodded at Dunn. The rest, as they say, was history.

Tom agreed to stay in the area until she was found and took me back to my house a little after five.

'I wouldn't half mind a coffee,' he said when we got in. 'Why don't you put the kettle on?'

'Why don't you?' I said. I felt I could afford to say it now.

'Because I need to take a leak. Stupid expression,' he continued as he made for the stairs. 'How can you *take* a leak? But that's the Americans for you.'

I'd just turned the tap on when I heard a thump upstairs. I turned the tap off, put the kettle down and went back into the living-room.

'Tom . . .?' then I heard him coming down.

She appeared at the bottom of the stairs. In her hand, Tom's gun was pointing at my midriff.

Chapter 19

'Back, Sister.'

'What have you done to Tom?'

'Back.' She gesticulated with the gun and I shifted a couple of paces. 'D'you have string?'

She must have knocked him out. 'I — no . . .'

'Tape?'

'Only Sellotape,' I said, remembering how we hadn't bothered to set a marker on the door.

'Where?'

'In the kitchen.'

'Get it, quickly.'

She followed me to the door and watched as I took the roll from the drawer.

'Upstairs, to the bathroom. Quickly.'

I went as slowly as I dared, in case there was a chance he might recover, but he was stretched on the floor, not moving. Beside him lay the bottle of bath salts she must have hit him with.

'Tape his wrists,' she ordered.

'I ought to check his pulse.'

'After you've taped him. Go on. I'm watching you.'

Taping a person up is not something I've had much experience with, so I didn't have to pretend to fumble.

'Make it tighter than that,' she ordered. 'Wind it round between his wrists and pull it tight. Go on, do it.'

I passed the roll between his arms a couple of times and pulled, tightening the turns I'd already made.

'Harder . . . Now make it fast.'

She threw me a pair of nail scissors, then told me to move back while she checked it.

'Now his feet. Go on.'

I repeated the performance on his ankles.

'Now drag him downstairs.'

'How can I —?'

'You've had enough practice moving patients, Sister. Do it.'

I put my hands under his shoulders and pulled. He was heavier than he looked, but I managed to get him through the door and to the top of the stairs.

'I'll go down first; you pull him after.'

'But what if —?'

'Just do it.'

I wondered for a moment about pulling him hard

enough to send us both rolling into her, but she went down nearly to the bottom.

'Go on, pull him.'

It was as he bumped over the first step that he let out a small groan and I felt a surge of relief — at least he was still alive.

She made me drag him to the middle of the floor before telling me to sit on the sofa.

'Lean back . . . that's right.'

It was the first chance I'd had to look at her properly. She was the same, superficially. The same flat features and mousy hair, still the same quiet voice, although there was a new edge to it now . . . but the main difference was in her eyes; they met mine defiantly, as though she was challenging me, trying to stare me down.

I felt compelled to say something. I said, 'They're going to find you sooner or later, Susan. Why make it worse for yourself?'

Her lips moved slightly in what might have been a smile.

'How could it be any worse?'

What could I say without provoking her?

'Susan, if you give yourself up, I promise I'll try and help you. I won't make anything of this' — I indicated Tom and the gun — 'and I'll be a witness on your behalf.'

'I'd still go to prison.'

Now, the difficult bit . . .

'I don't think so, Susan.'

This time she really did smile.

'You mean a hospital. A so-called hospital. For the insane. There's only one problem there, Sister — I'm not mad. I've known perfectly well what I was doing from the start.'

My tongue touched my lips. They felt very dry. Keep her talking. They like to talk . . .

'Why *did* you do it, Susan?'

'Somebody had to.'

'But why?'

'You *know* why.'

'I don't, really.'

She blinked rapidly a few times, then took a breath and she began, haltingly at first: 'Everything's a mess. Corrupt. The whole world. This country. People in Africa starving, but the richer we get, the more greedy we get. It all springs from selfishness and indulgence and greed . . .' Her eyes slid away from me for a moment, her mouth still open; I tensed, but as though she'd felt it, her eyes flicked back to me.

'I agree with you, Sus —'

'Do you? Are you any better than the rest?' She sucked in a breath. 'Oh, perhaps you are, a bit. It all comes down to Godlessness, you see. Greed comes from Godlessness. People look around and think that what they see is all there is, so they try and snatch as much of it as they can for themselves. While people can *see* God, they are reminded of their duties, their obligations; they stay on the path and — I suppose you think this is funny?'

I never felt less like laughing in my life.

'No, Susan, I don't, but —'

Her eyes gleamed with a momentary cunning. 'You're just saying that because you're frightened I might kill you, too.'

'Of course I'm frightened, but I said it because I understand, and —'

'Understand what?'

'What you mean, and why you did the things you —'

'I *had* to.' She spoke with a sudden change of emphasis, like a teacher speaking to a child. 'A person may lose God, that happens, but it's a thing to be sorry about, ashamed of. To be silent about, not to boast . . . These people, by proclaiming their Godlessness, they undermine those who waver, who might otherwise have found God again and . . .' She broke off, her lips opening slightly and shutting a few times.

I said, 'Susan, if you give yourself up and explain that, then no harm will come to you. I can promise you that.'

Again, the fleeting look of cunning. 'But my work. I wouldn't be able to continue my work . . .'

I closed my eyes for a moment, then said, 'Susan, do you really think that God wants you to go on killing people?'

'Of course.' No hesitation. 'It says so in the Bible.' Then, slowly, almost like a mantra: 'The wages of sin is death. Death.'

I swallowed. 'But —'

The phone rang.

I looked at her.

She said, 'Don't answer it.'

'They know she's here,' said a man's voice. Tom. 'They'll only come round looking for her if she doesn't answer it.'

Her tongue touched her lips. 'Tell them you were in the bath. You'll ring back later.'

I stretched over and picked it up.

'Hello?'

'Sister Farewell?'

'Yes?'

'Took yer time, didn't you?' Sutton.

'I was in the bath.'

'Sorry. Is Jones there?'

'No, I'm afraid she isn't.'

'I said, is *Jones* there?'

'I know. She's not here. I think she's on a nursing shift.'

'You aw right?'

'No, I'm not' — Susan was gesticulating — 'I must go now. I'll tell her you rang if she contacts me. Goodbye.' I put the phone down.

'Who was it?' Susan demanded.

'A boyfriend of Mary's. Sister Tamworth.'

'Why did he ring here?'

'He'd tried her flat, and she's often here.'

'You told them she was on duty. She's not on duty . . .'

'I know. It was all I could think of.'

'She's profane — Sister Tamworth.'

'She's . . . lost,' I said.

She sat back in her chair and looked at us in silence. Tom's gun in her hand never wavered. I hoped that Tom wouldn't say anything more . . .

He said, 'You realize that someone's going to look for us sooner or later?'

'Yes. By then, I will be gone.'

Panic was beginning to steal over me. 'D'you want us to help you, Susan?'

'You will help me,' she said flatly.

'Yes.'

'Do you have a passport?'

'Yes.'

'How old?'

'Er — five years.'

'Where is it?'

'In my desk. Upstairs.'

'Credit cards?'

'Yes.'

'How many?'

'Two.'

'Car documents?'

'Yes.'

She said, 'Is that your natural hair colour?'

'Almost.' I'd said it before I realized what she was getting at.

'So you've got some hair dye?'

Sick, appalled, I said, 'Not dye, no. A tinting compound, that's all.'

'We'll go up and look. Now.'

After a moment's hesitation, I got to my feet. I was shaking all over. She waved me forward with the gun. I went upstairs. Would Tom be able to work himself free . . .?

Into the bathroom.

'All my hair things are in there,' I said, indicating the wall cabinet. My voice was shaking too.

'Open it.'

I did so. She pushed the contents aside, knocking some to the floor. No dye.

'It doesn't matter. I'll get some later.'

'Susan' — I couldn't stop myself — 'are you going to kill us?'

'Why should I do that? I just need to get away from this area.'

I pretended to believe her. I might have actually believed her were it not for the pure animal cunning that fleeted through her eyes again . . .

She made me find my passport and other documents and we were at the top of the stairs when the doorbell rang.

She stiffened. 'Who would that be?'

'I don't know.'

'Sister Tamworth's boyfriend?'

'It could be.'

Her mouth opened and closed again.

'Don't let them in. Say you're not well, whoever it is.'

We went down the stairs. Tom didn't seem to have moved. Our eyes met as I passed him on the way to the door, Susan behind me.

'Remember,' she hissed, 'I've got nothing to lose.' She moved behind the door.

My hand was on the latch as the bell pealed again. I opened the door on to the chain.

It was Polo.

'I'm so sorry to disturb you, Sister,' he said. 'Mr Sutton sent me. He wants to see Mr Jones.' He sounded abnormally polite.

'Well, I'm afraid he's not here' — what could I say to alert him? 'John.'

'Oh. Do you know where I might find him, please?'

'I think he's gone back to London, John.'

'Do you have an address? Phone number?'

'I'm afraid not. But you should find him at the Department of Health in London.'

'I'll try that, then. So sorry to have bothered you, Sister.'

'That's all right. Bye, John.'

I shut the door. Swayed with dizziness. Susan's eyes were like stones.

'Go over to the window. Has he gone?'

'Yes.'

'Who was he? Why didn't he phone?'

'I'll tell you who it was!' I shouted, having decided attack was the only defence. 'That was . . . John' — I'd nearly said Polo — 'Len Sutton's man. You know who Len Sutton is? The husband of the Mrs Sutton you killed. He'll kill you without thinking about it if he finds you . . .'

'How does he know Mr Jones?'

'Because he was after you himself and we went round to his house to tell him to lay off, that's why.'

It seemed to satisfy her. She said, 'Lie down on the floor, next to him.'

My pulse missed a beat — was this it?

'Susan, I —' Then I saw that she'd picked up the Sellotape. I lay down. She put her knee in the small of my back and taped my hands. She was quite heavy and stronger than she looked. There was nothing I could do.

Tom said, 'You know they're going to get you in the end, don't you, Susan?'

'Oh, shut *up*, Jones!' I said.

'But I think she ought to know that,' he said reasonably.

'It's in God's hands,' Susan said.

'But doesn't God help those who help themselves.'

'I don't like to hear His name on your lips,' she said, dangerously quiet.

'I'm sorry —'

'I must continue to do His work for as long as He will allow me. It's in His hands.'

'But He wouldn't want you to kill a true believer, would He?'

'Tom, please be quiet,' I said.

'But I think this is important. He wouldn't want you to kill a true believer, would He, Susan?'

'But you're not a believer. Not a *true* believer.'

'Perhaps I'm not. But Sister Farewell is.'

She looked at me. 'Are you, Sister?'

'Er — yes, I believe I am.'

She poked her face close to mine. 'When did you last perform an act of worship? When did you last enter the house of God?'

'Yesterday. I went to St Chad's Cathedral.'

Her mouth worked silently, then, 'You're lying. What time?'

'It was just after five. There was a service — it was Thanksgiving.'

She stared at me. Her mouth opened to say something — closed — opened again.

'It's true,' Tom said loudly. 'I was there, waiting outside —'

'What was that noise?' She was on her feet.

'The window!' Tom said.

She turned to it . . . Polo appeared in the kitchen door . . . She whirled round, saw him, levelled the gun at my eyes . . . I wanted to close them, but couldn't . . . Saw her finger tighten, then a knife sliced into her hand as the gun went off . . . I remember thinking: I heard the bang, didn't I? That means I'm still alive, doesn't it . . .?

Chapter 20

Tom and Susan were taken to the hospital when the police arrived; Susan under guard. Polo and I were taken to the police station to give statements. We were joined by Sutton, and later by Tom, who'd been examined for concussion and discharged on condition he took it easy and didn't drive. Afterwards, we were all taken back to my house and it seemed only polite to ask Sutton and Polo inside.

'I knew she was going to kill us,' Tom said, 'which is why I risked speaking when the phone went.' The dressing round his head made him look vaguely Arabian. 'I was hoping you'd think of something to alert them at the other end, Jo, and you did.'

We were in the living-room. Tom and Polo were drinking tea: Tom because of his head, Polo because he had to drive. Sutton and myself had whisky.

'It was lucky it was you, Mr Sutton,' I said. 'I don't think I'd have been able to make anyone else understand.'

'Don't undersell yourself,' said Tom. 'You thought pretty quickly on your feet when Polo called.'

Sutton had sent Polo round to find out what was going on. After speaking to me, he'd got into his car and driven away, then walked back to the house next door and persuaded them to ring the police while he went through the back and forced my kitchen window.

'That's when I heard him,' said Tom. 'Which is why I started blathering — to keep her attention on me while Polo got through.'

'Climbin' through kitchen windows without makin' a noise ain't so easy,' Polo said feelingly.

'No,' agreed Tom. 'Although I'd have thought you'd have had enough practice.'

'Funny guy,' sneered Polo. 'Don't push it, man.'

'Sorry, Polo. Like I said earlier: we owe you. And that was the most beautiful piece of knife work I've seen in my life.'

Polo shrugged, but looked pleased.

'Shame it wasn't her neck,' Sutton muttered. He'd been morose and distant from the moment he'd arrived at the police station.

Tom turned to him. 'If it had been her neck, Miss Farewell would probably be dead. She was shooting to

216

kill, and hitting her hand to deflect her aim was the only way of stopping her.'

I hadn't realized that. 'Thanks, Polo,' I said.

''S aw right, Sister,' he said awkwardly.

'Sorry, Sister,' said Sutton. 'I didn't mean it that way.'

'That's all right,' I said, just as awkwardly. Although in a sense, Sutton, too, had saved our lives, there was no way I could feel comfortable with him, not after what he'd done to me that night in ITU.

'I still think she should be dead, though,' he continued now.

'It'll be worse for her in prison,' Tom said.

'That's what they always say.' He paused. ''Sides, she won't go to prison, will she? It'll be one o' them so-called hospitals, won't it?'

Tom looked at him sharply. 'Don't even think about it, Len,' he said. 'It ain't worth it. Revenge is always empty, and they'd get you for it anyway.'

He sighed heavily. 'Yeah, I suppose you're right,' he said. Not long after this, they both left.

'Would you like something to eat?' I asked as soon as they'd gone. We hadn't eaten for hours, and I was afraid he might want to go back to his hotel now that the immediate danger had passed.

'Might not be a bad idea,' he said. 'Thanks.'

I went into the kitchen and put on the kettle. It was the first moment I'd been in a room, any room, by myself since Polo had broken in and rescued us and my mind started winding back . . .

Susan had let out the most earsplitting screams while Polo retrieved first the gun, then his knife.

'No, Polo,' Tom had shouted, 'cut us free!'

He told me later he thought Polo had been on the point of killing her.

'Would he have, really?' I asked.

'He might. Remember, he knew the police were on their way, so it was his only chance. And it was what Sutton would have wanted.'

'She was going to try and take my place, wasn't she?' I said.

'And she might have got away with it long enough to get abroad. If Sutton hadn't phoned.'

It was rather ironic. He'd heard of her escape on the radio and was ostensibly phoning to offer help, although as Tom said, he was probably only looking for a chance to get his hands on her.

'Well, he won't be able to now, will he?'

'If I were Anslow,' Tom said slowly, 'I'd keep a careful eye on friend Sutton. He may have saved us, incidentally, but that doesn't make him a goody.'

One of the most shocking things was that as I'd tried to bind Susan's hands, she'd bitten me, drawing blood. Polo had knocked her out at that point with a blow to the neck and she'd still been unconscious when the police arrived . . .

ANDREW PUCKETT

I let out a shuddering sigh. I wasn't at all hungry myself. Some sense of irony caused me to make beans on toast for Tom, and when I put them in front of him with another mug of tea, he looked at them, then smiled wryly up at me. It was a smile that brought a lump to my throat. I sat down beside him.

Perhaps because it was the two of us again, my mind switched back to the moment Susan had pointed the gun at me, at *me*, not Polo, and pulled the trigger . . .

I began to shake again. He put his arm around me and I buried my face in his chest and bawled my eyes out. He held me, comforted me, and gradually, I became calmer again.

Then, there was this moment when comfort became something else. I looked up into his face, reached up and gently kissed his mouth. He looked down at me, swallowed. I kissed him again, softly, then harder. Perhaps I shouldn't have, but at that moment, my need was the greater. The beans grew cold. We went upstairs.

*

I woke the next morning to find him already up and staring out of the bedroom window.

'Feeling guilty?' I asked him lightly.

He turned. 'A bit.'

'I can't believe that this is the first time you've cheated on your wife.'

'As a matter of fact, it is.'

'I'm . . . sorry.'

He smiled. 'It takes two.'

We had some breakfast, then went down to the police station to see Anslow. He was looking tired, but pleased.

'Well, she's admitted everything,' he told us. 'Plus five others she killed before you spotted her, Sister.'

'Five?'

'Oh yes . . .'

She'd started some months earlier when she heard a particularly macho patient boasting of his atheism after he'd recovered from a heart attack, and then hearing the voice of God telling her that unbelievers, being the worst kind of sinners, deserved to have their wages paid in full. She also claimed that it was God who had suggested pressurizing the vacutainer bottles.

'Although I suspect she's plugging the God angle for all it's worth, with an eye to a plea of diminished responsibility,' Anslow observed.

That first killing had been so easy that she'd decided to look for more sinners. She called up the patient record system on the laboratory terminal when there was no one around and noted the names of the unbelievers, i.e. atheists, agnostics or none. She then used one of her pre-pressurized sample bottles when next she bled them.

She knew that the nurse in Thatchbury had been caught through the examination of staff rotas, so she varied the types of insulin she'd used so as to vary the times of death after administration, reasoning that that, and the comparatively large number of staff on ITU, plus the already high death rate, would cover her activities.

She'd killed Mrs Sutton with PZI after returning from leave because, as Tom had said, she was the wife of a gangster, and she'd attempted suicide.

'I'll tell you something funny,' Anslow said. 'I'm certain in my own mind that part of her knew that the trap we set up for her *was* a trap.'

'You mean, she wanted to be caught?' I asked.

He took a breath. 'Yes and no. Serial killers tend to get to a point when their killings begin to sicken even them, and yet they know they'll never stop. So they take ever greater risks, stop being careful. In a sense, they give up.'

'But she was still talking about the voice of God to us, wasn't she, Tom?'

'But did it mean anything by then?' Tom said.

'It sounded as though it did, to me.'

'Well, I'll tell you something else,' Anslow continued. He paused a moment to gather his thoughts. 'When I was interviewing her last night, I really did feel, more than I ever have before, that I was getting answers from two completely different people.' He sighed. 'Or maybe I was just tired. Anyway, it's for the trick cyclists to sort out now.'

Just as we left, he said, 'Oh, Sister, I think these are

yours.' He was holding out the keys I'd lost. 'We found them in her pocket.'

*

I saw Tom off on the afternoon train. He gave me one of those kisses somehow so filled with possibility that I almost tried persuading him to stay. But it wouldn't have been fair on him. Or his wife. That's what I told myself, anyway.

The next day, I went back to work.

Immediately after the ward rounds, Mr Chorley called me to his office. He told me how sorry he was and that I was to come to him if I had any problems. He then ordered me to take a week off and I felt a lump grow in my throat at his kindness.

When I got back to my own office, Miss Whittington was there waiting for me. She apologized for not believing me earlier. She sounded as though she'd been kicked from above.

Some of the others, like Mary, were obviously dying to ask me all about it, but had just enough sensitivity not to. It would come later, I was sure.

Stephen caught me alone as I was on the point of leaving. 'Jo, I can't tell you how sorry I am; I can't find the words to apologize sufficiently . . .'

There was more in the same vein, then he astounded me by saying: 'I'd really like to make it up to you, Jo. Let me take you out for dinner. Tomorrow, perhaps?'

And the amazing thing was that he honestly seemed to think it was that easy. Words tumbled round my head, like: *Where were you when I needed you? . . . Fair-weather friend . . . Go back to Jill and Debbie*, but what actually came out was: 'Stephen, go and stick it up your arse.' Followed by: 'And if you think there's a double meaning there, you're right.'

He didn't redden or look away, just smiled faintly for a moment, then turned and left.

I spent the next couple of days with my parents, playing down what had happened and trying to put their minds at rest.

Tom phoned me on Wednesday to say that he was coming up the next day to collect his car; also to attend the magistrates' court where Susan was due to appear, in case there were any more developments Anslow could tell him about.

I decided to go with him, partly out of morbid curiosity, I suppose, but mostly because I wanted to see him again.

It was cold and windy, no autumnal mellowness that day. Anslow couldn't tell us any more, other than that their case was virtually complete, and that Sutton had been well and truly warned off.

The court appearance was an anticlimax. We were inside (with Sutton, who'd attached himself to us) when she was brought to the building in a police van. We could hear the relatives of some of the dead patients shouting abuse at her as she arrived. When she appeared in the court, she looked no different from the way she'd always looked. I don't know what I'd expected.

She said 'Yes' twice — once to confirm her name and again to say she understood the charges. Then it was over.

We were outside by the time she was brought back to the van. I was expecting her to have a blanket or something over her head, but she didn't. More abuse was shouted. A ring of police surrounded her.

The wind was gusting more than ever, plucking at her hair and coat — no, they were *bullet* holes, followed immediately by the reports of the gunshots . . .

Chapter 21

As the echoes died away, there was a moment of absolute silence and stillness, then, like a film starting up again, people began to move . . .

Police running in the direction of the shots . . .

Tom turning to Sutton and saying, 'You bloody fool . . .'

Then me, pushing my way through the crowd — 'Excuse me, please, I'm a nurse . . .'

She was lying on her back, the blood flowing from beneath her. I felt for her pulse, and to my amazement, there was one, although very weak. I made pads from the lining of my jacket and manoeuvred them underneath her back where I thought the exit wounds would be, moving her as little as possible. Then I covered her with coats from the bystanders . . .

Her face remained completely still. The crowd around me gobbled like a turkey farm.

Then, the wail of the ambulance and the crowd parting to let the paramedics through. I offered to go with them, but they said it wasn't necessary. Tom joined me as they drove away.

'Is she still alive?'

'Yes, but I wouldn't give much for her chances. Have they caught them?'

'They've arrested Sutton.'

'But why? It couldn't have been him, he was with us the whole time.'

'They think he hired whoever did it.'

'And then came here to watch? How revolting.'

'He said he hadn't, just before Anslow arrested him.'

'Did you believe him?'

He shook his head slightly. 'I don't think so. No.' He looked up. 'I asked Anslow if I could sit in, but he said no.'

I smiled wryly and told him how my offer of help had been spurned too.

He said, 'There was something else I wanted to talk to you about. Is there anywhere we can go?'

'Only my place.'

By the time we got to his car, reaction had set in and neither of us spoke on the way back. When we arrived, I said, 'I'm sorry, but I must have a coffee. D'you want one?'

'Please.'

'What was it you wanted to talk to me about?' I asked when I'd made it.

'It's probably not important.' He took a mouthful. 'The thing is, I've never been happy about the numbers of atheists and agnostics that suddenly descended on your ITU.'

I shrugged. 'We just happened to have a lot of them in that period.'

'If you hadn't, you probably wouldn't have noticed the killings.'

'Why not?' I wasn't really concentrating.

'Because they wouldn't have been killed.'

'Oh. I hadn't thought of that.'

'Well, while I was back in London, I contacted three local ITUs and asked them how many non-believers they had.' He smiled. 'They made the same observation as I: that patients coming into an ITU, and their relatives, tend to rediscover their religious faith, not lose it. Anyway, the rate came out as one in nineteen, near enough. In your case, the rate over that period was one in seven.'

'Is that so very different?' I asked.

'It certainly is. It means your ITU had nearly three times as many as the others I've looked at, and that's statistically significant. In other words, it didn't happen by chance.'

'Tom, what are you saying?'

'I'm not really sure.' He hesitated. 'Anslow suggested that Susan has a split personality. Could one part of her have changed the patient records for the other part of her to find? That was another reason I came up here, to find out whether that could have happened.'

I thought about it. 'But as a phlebotomist, she didn't have a password.'

'We already know she was using someone else's password to look at the files.'

I drank the rest of my coffee.

'It all depends on whether you're right about the number of unbelievers,' I said. 'I'm not convinced you are.'

'Well, there's one way to find out.'

'How?'

'By going back to ITU and checking how many non-believing patients you had outside the period Susan was killing them.'

We picked at some lunch before going back at half-past one, when I hoped there wouldn't be so many people about.

The first person we saw was Mary.

'Jo! What are you doing here? Aren't you on leave?'

'Just something I had to sort out.'

'You know Susan's in theatre?'

I nodded. 'Yes.'

'Were you there? Did you see it happen?'

'Yes.' I briefly told her about it. 'Are we expecting her here?'

'Yes. One of the side rooms has been prepared.'

'OK. I'll be staying for a little while, so let me know when she arrives, please.'

Tom and I went into my office, where it didn't take us long to work out that our usual rate of 'non-believers' was one in twenty-one.

'It could still be a fluke, a coincidence,' I said.

'It isn't, Jo, and you know it. And there's a way we can prove it.'

'How?'

'By asking the relatives.'

'Oh, no.' I shook my head. 'No. That would be a completely unjustifiable intrusion.'

'Why?'

'Because you can't —'

There was a tap on the door. Mary.

'She's come out of theatre, and Inspector Anslow is here,' she said. We could see him behind her.

'How is she?'

'Alive. That's all I know.'

'Thanks, Mary. Inspector,' I called, 'would you like to come in?'

His large presence seemed to make the office even smaller.

'She's still alive, then. What're the chances, Sister?'

'I won't know that until I've spoken to one of the doctors. I'll do that once she's here.'

He nodded, then said feelingly, 'I hope to God she does survive.'

Tom said, 'Did you get anywhere with Sutton?'

'Nah,' he said in disgust. 'He got his solicitor in, denied

all knowledge and we couldn't prove otherwise, so we had to let him go. We're still holding his minder, though.'

'Polo? You don't think it was him? He's a knifeman, not a gunman.'

'You're probably right,' said Anslow gloomily. 'But he could have been the intermediary, so maybe we can break him.'

Tom looked doubtful about that, and I could understand why.

'So you still think Sutton was behind it?'

Anslow snorted. 'Who else could it be?'

'Have you found out where the gunman was yet?'

'An empty office about a hundred yards away. Forensic are still working on it.'

'Cartridge cases?'

He nodded. 'Three. From a treble-two bolt action.'

'Three . . . so he missed with one of the shots?'

'Looks like it.' He obviously didn't want to say any more about it.

Tom said after a pause, 'Remember your idea that she had a split personality?'

'Well?'

'Has any more been said about that?'

'A psychiatrist has been to see her, but I haven't heard anything. Why?'

Tom told him about the patient records. 'We're wondering whether one part of her altered them for the other to find.'

'Hmm, interesting. I'll ask and let you know.'

As soon as he'd gone, Tom phoned Sutton.

'Can we come round and see you?' he asked without preamble.

There was an angry crackle from the other end.

'No,' Tom said. 'We just want to talk to you. It's important.'

He arranged for us to go round in half an hour and rang off.

I said, 'What makes you think I want to go with you?'

'Don't you?'

In fact, I did, and after making sure everything was running smoothly, we went.

The other minder, the white one, let us in, then frisked us before admitting us to the living-room. Sutton stood up as we came in.

'Well, what d'you want?'

It struck me again how much he'd aged.

'Can we sit down?' said Tom.

Sutton shrugged and we sat. After a moment, Tom said, '*Was* it you, Len?'

'No.'

'Who was it, then?'

'No idea.'

'All right. Any idea which hitman they'd use?'

He reflected for a moment. 'There're three in the West Midlands I know of. Weren't any of them, though.'

'How d'you know that?'

He snorted. 'She's still alive, ain't she?'

'So why did you go along today?'

This time, he took longer before answering.

'I thought about what you said, about how she'd suffer more alive in prison than dead. The emptiness of revenge. That's why I didn't do it.'

'But —'

'Oh, I'll not be sorry if she dies, but I didn't do it.' His eyes turned away. 'But I had to see her for myself. I'll go to the trial too, if she survives.'

After a moment, Tom heaved a sigh and stood up. 'Thanks for your time, Len. They'll have to let Polo out soon. They've got nothing on him.'

As soon as we were in the car, I said, 'Did you believe him?'

'Yes. I'd begun to wonder anyway.'

'Why?'

'Sutton would have hired the best, and I don't think the best would have used a treble-two. They certainly wouldn't have missed with one of the shots, and, as Sutton said, she wouldn't still be alive.'

'But who else could it have been? One of the relatives?'

'Possibly.' He paused, thinking. 'Let's go back and check the religions of those patients.'

I told him how much I didn't like it, but then he said he'd do it himself, so I capitulated.

It wasn't quite as bad as I'd feared. I managed to contact relatives of four of the original seven, only one of whom showed any resentment.

Three of the dead patients had been Church of England, one of them a regular churchgoer, and the other a Methodist. In no case would they, or their relatives, have described them as atheist or agnostic, or even as none.

'So the records were altered,' said Tom, stating the obvious. 'But by whom? Do you have a computer department here?'

'Yes.'

'Well, they should have a record of the password used to make the alterations.'

He phoned them and we both went round. Once his authority had been established, they checked their own records. The religion had been altered on all seven patients, and in each case, the password was the same: MET 253. Mary Elizabeth Tamworth.

*

'I still can't believe it,' I said. We were on our way back to ITU.

'Why not?'

'What possible motive could she have?'

'Let's ask her, shall we?'

She was on the ward. I phoned through and asked her to come to my office.

An anomaly had arisen, I said to her, that needed checking out, and told her about the altered records, but not their significance.

'Well, I didn't do it,' she said, and I would have sworn the surprise on her face was genuine. 'Why should I have?'

'Can you prove that?' Tom asked.

'Yes, I think I can. Let me see those dates again.' The red spots of anger had appeared on her cheeks.

Tom handed them over.

'I thought so. This date, September the twenty-seventh. I had a day's leave and spent it in Birmingham.'

'Any witnesses?'

'Yes. D'you want their names?'

Tom checked it out after she'd gone and it was true.

'So we're back to the same question,' he said. 'Did Susan alter the records, or was it someone else?'

It was something we'd never be able to ask her because she died that night without regaining consciousness.

Chapter 22

The next morning, as soon as we heard the news, Tom made two phone calls — a short one to Anslow, and a longer one to his boss in London. When he finished, he came into the kitchen where I was percolating some coffee.

'Want some?' I asked.

'Thanks. Anslow's spoken to the shrink who interviewed Susan. He thinks it's extremely unlikely she would have altered any patient notes herself.'

'So who did?'

'That remains to be seen. I've arranged for us to visit the British Transplant Headquarters in London this afternoon, so —'

'I wish you'd asked before arranging these things for me,' I said snappishly.

'I thought you'd want to come.'

I realized that I did. Maybe detection is like a drug, or — more likely perhaps — having been there at the beginning, I wanted to see it through to the end.

'I just wish you'd ask first,' I said rather lamely.

He grinned. 'Sorry, force of habit. Jo, I'd *like* you to come. Your impressions would be very useful. I ask the questions, and you watch the reactions.'

'Whose reactions?' I asked, despite myself.

'I hope, the people who allocated the organs from your patients.'

We went in his car.

It was a good two-hour journey and at first, we sat in silence. I'd wanted him to come back to my house (and to my bed) the previous evening, but now, perversely, I felt used.

After a while, I asked him about his wife. He told me her name was Holly. I asked him what she was like.

I don't know why I did, unless it was some form of masochism. Oh, I wasn't in love with him or anything, I would have just liked . . .

It was just that after Stephen, he seemed so . . . well, desirable.

Rebound?

Maybe. I don't know.

The British Transplant HQ was in central London and he found his way there easily, even somewhere to park.

Professor Barnett, the director, was a tall, scholarly

man of about sixty with gold-rimmed glasses. He had a pronounced stoop and when he sat, you could see that the top of his head was bald beneath the hair scraped over it.

'How can I help you?' he asked. 'Your superior, Mr Evans, seemed to think that the matter was of some urgency.'

You could tell from his tone that he hadn't liked being pushed to see us, but was too much of a gent to say so directly.

'That's right, Professor,' Tom said cheerfully, as apparently thick-skinned as ever. 'Over the last two months or so, several patients have died in suspicious circumstances at St Chad's hospital in Latchvale — that's how come Sister Farewell here is involved. A large proportion of them donated their organs and, to complete the investigation, I've been given the job of tracing what happened to them.'

'I see,' said the professor, his eyes never leaving Tom's face. 'What do you mean, exactly, by *suspicious circumstances*?'

Tom glanced at me as though deciding how much to say, although we'd already done so.

'It seems that they were murdered, Professor.'

'Good heavens! How appalling . . .'

'The perpetrator has been apprehended, but we now need to tie up every loose end in the case.'

'I see,' he said again, thoughtfully. 'How many patients were — er — murdered?'

'We know of thirteen definitely — although there may be more.'

'And how many of these . . .?'

'Donated their organs? Of the thirteen, seven that we're interested in.'

'And you want to know where their organs went?'

'That's right. It would also be a help if you could outline for us the way organs are allocated, and after that, perhaps we could meet the people who are actually in charge of allocating them.'

'I see,' the professor said, for the third time. 'Mr Jones, is there more to this inquiry than you have led me to believe?'

'Not so far as I know,' Tom lied blandly. 'The culprit was obviously insane — I say was, because she has been killed, apparently by one of the relatives, before she could be fully examined by a psychiatrist. That's why it's so important for us to examine every detail concerning the patients she killed.'

'Mmm.' He took a breath. 'All right. Organ allocation. The name of every patient in the United Kingdom who needs a transplant is entered into our main frame computer, together with all their medical details, including their tissue type. When an organ becomes available, its tissue type is entered and the computer comes up with the best matches for it.

'However, it is not necessarily the patient with the best match who receives the organ. If there is another patient with a very good match who has an overriding need for the organ, say, for instance, they have only days or weeks to live without a transplant, then it might go to them.'

Tom leaned forwards. 'How is this decided?'

'One of our consultant staff here would discuss the matter with the patient's consultant. In some cases, I become involved. A lot would depend on the patient's availability, of course.'

'Of course.' Tom hesitated. 'And now, would it be possible to meet the members of your staff concerned, please?'

'If they are available, yes. Do you have a list of the patients' names?'

Tom handed it over.

There was a silence broken only by the tapping of the keys as the professor entered them. He was very good at it, I noticed. At last he said, 'There are two consultants involved, Doctors Potter and Enfield. You see,' he looked up, 'each of the seven patients donated three organs: two kidneys and a liver. For the past year or so, Dr Potter has been allocating livers; Dr Enfield, kidneys. Do you wish to see them both?'

I could see Tom thinking quickly, then he said, 'Yes, we would, please. And separately, if you wouldn't mind.'

'Separately? Why?'

'I think it would give us a clearer picture of how the particular allocations are made.'

'I don't see how. Mr Jones, are you sure you've told me everything? Is one of my staff under any kind of —?'

'Professor,' Tom interrupted firmly. 'As I said earlier, this is a loose end which has to be tied up. Eliminated, if you like. For the moment, I think it's better if we leave it at that.'

The two men looked at each other for a moment before Barnett said, 'Very well,' and I wondered at the clout of Tom's boss. Medical directors of any sort don't usually back down that easily.

Tom continued, 'I think it might be better if we saw them in a room other than their own offices. And we'll need the printouts of each of the transplant allocations so that we can study the details first.'

*

Dr Malcolm Potter was a dark, somewhat overweight man with a bushy beard that covered at least half his face. He wore glasses with thick tinted lenses, and his hand felt clammy as I shook it.

'Livers tend to be a more tricky prospect transplant-wise than kidneys,' he explained, 'from the point of view of allocation as well as the operation itself.' He went on to tell us about his method of allocating the organs, which was much as Barnett had described.

'What can you tell us about these?' Tom handed him a copy of the list of patients.

Potter glanced at it. 'Not very much, without my

computer. I take it these are donors of organs we've handled?'

'Yes. Use this terminal. I know Professor Barnett won't mind.' We were in the professor's room.

'Oh. Very well.' He tapped in a password, then the first of the names. 'Can I write on this list?'

'By all means.'

He started writing.

'Well,' he said at last. 'All seven of the livers were transplanted, and so far, three have been rejected.'

'Were they the best matches in each case?'

'Yes, excepting this one . . .' He showed us.

'Tell us about it,' said Tom.

The patient had been desperately in need of a transplant and the liver had been allocated to him although the match wasn't the best. It had subsequently been rejected and the patient had died.

'That's the whole problem,' Potter said. 'Do you give the organ to someone who'll definitely die without it, but who'll probably die anyway even with it? Or do you give it to someone who might make better use of it?'

'Whose decision was it in this case?' Tom asked.

'Mine, and Professor Barnett's. I asked him because the patient's consultant had put considerable pressure on me. The professor considered it justified in this case.'

'Did you think it justified?'

Potter hesitated. 'Is this strictly in confidence?'

'Absolutely.'

'Well, no, I didn't, as a matter of fact. But it's easy to be wise after the event, isn't it?'

'One last thing. How well do you know Miss Shenstone of St Chad's in Latchvale?'

'I've met her. I have great admiration for her. I can't say that I know her personally.'

*

Dr David Enfield couldn't have been more different. He was as tall and thin as Barnett, but erect, with a strong bony face and fair hair just beginning to turn grey. His manner was open and confident.

'Kidneys are often easier to allocate than the other organs,' he told us, 'because there are two of them. So if you're in the situation of having one patient with a very good match versus another with an overriding need, you can satisfy both.'

'Was it that easy in these seven cases?' Tom asked. He passed the list of patients over.

Enfield studied it. 'I'll have to consult the computer to tell you that.'

'Please, go ahead.'

Enfield went ahead and after a few minutes said, 'Yes, they were all pretty straightforward.'

'But what about this one?' Tom produced the printout of a more contentious case we'd noticed among those the professor had produced for us earlier: one recipient with a desperate need, and two others who had very good matches.

'How did you decide which of these two should have the kidney?' he asked.

'Ah, yes, this one was a difficult decision.' For the first time, I thought I detected a hint of nervousness about him. He continued: 'In the end, after studying both cases very carefully, I decided that one of them had a slightly greater priority.'

'Did you involve Professor Barnett in your decision?'

'No, I didn't. I saw no need to. I'm perfectly well qualified to take these decisions on my own.'

'Did you speak with both consultants involved?'

'Naturally. Look, I know you've got the director's go-ahead for these questions, but I must say, I can't understand the reason for them.'

'Just tying up loose ends, Doctor,' Tom said irritatingly. Enfield's lips tightened, but he didn't pursue it any further.

'D'you know Miss Shenstone at all?' Tom asked. 'Miss Marie Shenstone at St Chad's in Latchvale?'

'Of course I do. Everyone knows of her.'

'What I asked was, do you *know* her? To speak to.'

'I do, as a matter of fact. As do a great many people in this field.'

Chapter 23

As soon as Enfield had left us, Tom made a call from the pay phone in the corridor. Then we gathered together all the relevant printouts, thanked Professor Barnett and left for Tom's office in the Department of Health, in Whitehall.

His boss, Marcus Evans, was tall and spare, and one of the baldest men I have ever met. Perhaps to compensate for this, he had a heavy black moustache, which somehow gave humour to his face, as well as strength. He also had an old-fashioned charm and courtesy that made me warm to him immediately.

'Have you had lunch yet, Miss Farewell?'

'I haven't, actually.' It was half-past one and I was beginning to feel hungry.

'I thought you'd want to see what we've found first, Marcus,' Tom said.

Marcus looked up at his clock. 'If we don't go now, we won't get any,' he said. 'From what you told me on the phone, Tom, I think it could wait half an hour, don't you?' It was said with a smile, though, so that it wasn't a put-down.

We went to the staff refectory, where the food was excellent. I've noticed before that the administrators always manage to fix themselves up with better food than the doers. I didn't say so, though. Tom clearly wanted to talk about the case, but Marcus wasn't having any.

'Have you always lived in Latchvale, Miss Farewell?' he asked me.

'I was born there.'

'No desire to move away?'

'Not any more. I did a couple of years post registration in Birmingham, that was quite enough big city life for me.'

'I stayed there for a few days myself once — Latchvale, that is — visiting the hospital. There's more to it than Birmingham somehow, although it's so much smaller. History, perhaps. There's a cathedral with three spires, isn't there?'

'Yes, they're called the Ladies of the Vale,' Tom said knowledgeably.

Marcus looked faintly surprised. 'Miss Farewell's been showing you around?'

'Yes,' he said breezily. 'Attended a service, didn't we, Jo? Listened to the choir.'

Bloody liar, I thought.

'Hmm,' said Marcus. 'Ah well, better get back to the grind, I suppose. How did Holly feel about you rushing back to the Midlands yesterday, Tom?'

You bastard, I thought.

Tom said, 'Well, I had to go back to collect the car, and then all this came up.'

'Remarkably understanding girl, Holly.'

'Yes.'

Back in Marcus's office, Tom took him through what had happened in the last two days.

'Not really conclusive, is it?' Marcus said, tugging at his moustache.

'Not absolutely, no. But I think we can draw some conclusions, or at least, a hypothesis.'

'Please do.'

Tom cleared his throat. 'All right, but I tell it in my own way — agreed?'

We agreed.

'OK. The first point is that although Susan King started killing non-believers of her own volition, somebody else spotted this and manipulated her for their own ends. We know this because of the altered patient notes on the computer.

'Secondly, the motive for this has to be organ transplant, because of the statistics, the seven out of eight victims with organ donor cards.'

'But what about the five earlier killings,' Marcus said,

'the ones Miss Farewell didn't spot? Did they have organ donor cards?'

'No, because they were Susan all on her own. It was when someone realized what she was doing that they then chose victims with donor cards and altered their patient notes for her to find.'

'So who is this someone?'

'I'll come to that in a moment. The person behind the organ related killings must be Miss Shenstone.' He smiled mirthlessly. 'I got the idea while Jo was showing me the Ladies of the Vale. I know Jo thinks she's a saint, but she's the only one with the know-how.'

'What's her motive for doing this?'

'I thought you were going to let me tell this in my own way,' Tom protested, and Marcus gestured for him to continue.

'She has to be in collusion with someone at Transplant Headquarters, and I suggest that person is Enfield — because Enfield is dealing with kidneys, which are Shenstone's speciality, and because the one really contentious medical case we came across concerns him.

'I suggest the mechanism is this: *One*: Enfield makes a deal with a patient who needs a kidney. Their need might be urgent, although probably not desperate, and they'd obviously be well-heeled. He then gives Shenstone the tissue type of the potential donee.

'*Two*: Shenstone finds a patient at St Chad's who has

an organ donor card and a very good match with the donee —is there such a word as donee?'

'I think recipient is more usual.'

'All right, recipient. Anyway, it has to be a very good match so that the donee will automatically have the best claim. Shenstone knows all the patients' tissue types because of the research she and Dr Cannock are doing. She tells Stephen Wall, who then alters the patient's notes, so that Susan King thinks they're an unbeliever and deals with them in the manner she deals with all unbelievers.

'*Three* —'

'Wait a minute, Tom, how on earth do you implicate Stephen Wall?'

'Please, Marcus, let me finish. *Three*: the kidney then becomes available for the donee. The computer at Transplant HQ shows it's the best match — which Enfield already knows, and if there's more than one claimant, as there was in the case we noticed, Enfield has to make his difficult decision.'

He sat back.

'So shoot me down.'

Marcus looked up from the notes he'd been scribbling.

'I met Miss Shenstone when I visited St Chad's. I don't know about her being a saint, but she did strike me as a remarkable, and a *good*, woman. So what's her motive?'

'Her department's in financial trouble.'

'Really? How did you find that out?'

I leaned forwards. I was quite interested to know myself.

'Last Saturday, when Jo was putting together all the staff rotas, I'd arranged a meeting with one of the finance administrators. He told me.'

'How much financial trouble?'

'Terminal. You see, there isn't really any justification for a small department like hers — she's only been allowed to keep it on because of the research she did, and her name. Once St Chad's becomes an NHS Trust, the board will insist that it becomes self-supporting, or closes down.'

'But why should she mind so much? She must be well into her sixties: you'd have thought she'd have just retired gracefully.'

'I wondered about that,' I put in.

'I agree,' said Tom. 'But a great many elderly people, especially those with a reputation, are unwilling to leave the stage when it actually comes to it. We've all come across them. I suggest that she's an extreme example.'

'We need more than just a suggestion of her unwillingness to retire, Tom.'

'All right, how about this? Her department has recently received two large, and anonymous, donations. I suspect that more are on their way, enough to keep the department afloat.'

'These are verifiable facts, are they, Tom? That her department's in financial trouble, but has been receiving anonymous donations?'

'Yes.'

'All right. How did she know that Susan was killing atheists?'

'Stephen Wall told her.'

'How did *he* know? I don't understand his involvement at all. What's *his* motive in this?'

'I think that it was Stephen Wall who realized what Susan was doing in the first place. I don't know exactly how, but he was in the right position to spot her. Shenstone and his father were at medical school together, but I think her relationship with Stephen is a lot closer than that. It must be if she can prime him with questions to ask her at an open lecture.'

'But that's not a motive. I'm not convinced about him, Tom.'

'Could I interrupt a moment, please?' I put in.

Marcus waved a hand for me to continue.

'I had a brief relationship with Stephen,' I said. 'It started just after I told him of my suspicions about the deaths. He persuaded me that my statistics were wrong, and then' — I swallowed — 'the relationship began. We saw each other for about two weeks, during which time there were no further deaths. We know now that this was because Susan was away on leave; however, I suggest the deaths would have stopped anyway. I'm also sure that Mrs Sutton's death was not intended, not by Stephen, anyway. That was Susan on her own, when she heard about Mrs Sutton. What I'm getting at is . . .' I swallowed again. I was hating this.

'Stephen only went out with me to allay my suspicions. When they returned, after Mrs Sutton was killed, he did his best to isolate me, make sure I would be ridiculed if I said anything.'

'Forgive me, Miss Farewell,' Marcus said gently, 'but I must ask you to be definite in your own mind about that. I'm sure this young man treated you very badly, but are you certain that there was any more to it than that?'

'Am I a woman scorned, you mean?' I said angrily. 'Well, I'm —'

'A *person* scorned,' he said.

I had to smile. 'I may have been, but there is more to it than that. Early in the week of Mrs Sutton's death, when I really needed someone, Stephen dropped me, just like that.' I heard my voice crack slightly as the nightmarish memory came back. 'But once Tom had come on the scene, and I had demonstrably pulled myself together, he suddenly couldn't keep away from me. At the time, I flattered myself that it was me he was concerned about, but now I think he was trying to find out about Tom. I think Tom's right about him.'

'It all fits,' Tom said. 'It was Shenstone who saw the potential of knowing the tissue types of all the patients . . .' His eyes flicked in their sockets as something else occurred to him . . . 'What if they had part of the racket working earlier, but only to the extent of guiding suitable kidneys the right way . . . I can just imagine Shenstone saying: *Mr Bloggs has the right tissue type, and he carries a donor card. What a shame he couldn't die* . . . and then Wall spots Susan . . .'

'You still haven't come up with a credible motive for Stephen Wall,' Marcus said.

'What about money?' I said, remembering. 'He wants to go into partnership with his father and build a private health centre. That costs money.'

'You know that, do you?'

'Yes.' I told him about our talk in Luigi's wine bar.

'That gives him both motive and opportunity,' said Tom. Marcus took a breath and sat back.

'Are you really convinced about this, Miss Farewell?' he asked me.

'Yes, I am. I did find Miss Shenstone's involvement hard to take at first, but it does all fit together now.'

'All right. One last thing' — he looked at Tom — 'why did they have Susan King killed, when she would have taken the blame for the killings?'

'Because sooner or later, she was going to be interrogated by experts, who would have then tried to verify every detail of her story. We've worked out how she was manipulated. They could have worked it out too.'

Marcus nodded slowly. 'So how do we go about

proving it? The police already have their killer; are they really going to want to believe this? It'll sound very far-fetched.'

'I think we can make a good case,' said Tom. 'All they need do is detain the three of them and let them stew while they grill every single patient who's had one of those kidneys, forgive my mixed culinary metaphors. One of them'll break down.'

'But what's to stop Enfield ringing them all and warning them?' I cried. 'He's probably already done it . . .'

Tom grinned wolfishly. 'If he does, great, because we've got his phone tapped. And if he doesn't —'

'When did you arrange that —? Oh, the phone call you made . . .'

'And if he doesn't,' Tom continued, 'we'll still get one of the donees to break down.'

Chapter 24

But it didn't work out that way.

Tom, with Marcus's backing, managed to convince Anslow that Miss Shenstone and Doctors Wall and Enfield (who hadn't made any incriminating phone calls) should be detained and left to stew while all the kidney recipients were rounded up. Potter was watched, just in case, although the liver patients were quickly eliminated from the inquiry.

But none of the fourteen kidney patients broke down. It became fairly obvious which ones were involved because, in Tom's words, they were well-heeled, and large amounts of money had recently been paid out of their accounts. Unfortunately, they all had stories ready to explain this.

Even when it was discovered that two of them shouldn't, on medical grounds, have been the ones to receive the kidneys in question (the other good matches having better medical cases), this couldn't be proved to be anything other than medical misjudgement.

The three doctors were comprehensively 'grilled', but none of them admitted anything, and after forty-eight hours, the police were forced to release them. All three immediately announced their intention to sue for wrongful arrest.

Tom, who'd stayed in the city (in a hotel with his wife) while all this was going on, seethed and spluttered like an angry steam engine.

'I've got a bloody good mind to tell Sutton,' he raged when they were released, and both Holly and I rounded on him.

'If you did that, I'd leave you,' Holly said. 'You're the one who's always said that people are innocent until proven guilty.'

'And I'd shop you,' I added.

It had been strange meeting Tom's wife. She was attractive (although older than me — about thirty, I guessed) and the antithesis of him. Considerate, slowly spoken and attentive to others.

He had introduced us with no trace of shame whatsoever, but I could see that she suspected something, if not actually knew.

And although she didn't much like it, she wasn't worried. She held — carried, rather — an overwhelming advantage. She was about seven months pregnant.

(Which, as I thought about it, might explain his susceptibility, and her forbearance.)

'No one would ever be able to prove anything if I did,' Tom muttered.

His feelings were understandable. He'd assured the police that it was all wrapped up, and when they'd had to release the three doctors, they were very cross with him, especially when they were threatened with legal action. They referred to him as an 'interfering amateur' (the worst possible insult) and the credibility of his department was compromised.

'Tom,' I said to him before they left, 'are they likely to . . . try and get revenge?'

He smiled. 'Don't worry about that. I know that's easy to say, but I've never heard of it happening, not in circumstances like these.'

'But the hitman who killed Susan . . .'

'Listen. The three of them have had a very near escape. The threat of legal action is just that: a threat, another way of protesting their innocence. Believe me, they won't do *anything* which might put them at risk again.'

'I hope you're right.'

'I am, you'll see.' His face darkened again. 'Anyway, I haven't finished with them yet. Marcus has told me I can go on digging for a while. It's not over yet.'

That was just bravado, I was sure. I saw them both off shortly afterwards.

It isn't the same place, I thought after I'd gone back into my little house and sat down in the silence.

I looked around.

This is where Tom had slept — at first, anyway. Over there, by the door, is where Sutton and Polo had forced their way in and threatened me.

And here is where I'd broken down, got drunk and felt my reason slipping away when Stephen betrayed me . . . And just there is where Susan tried to kill me . . .

I gave a sigh and went into the kitchen to make some coffee. It would wear off. If it didn't, I'd have to move. Give it a few more weeks.

A couple of days later, I was officially back at work, where my curiosity value only lasted a couple of hours, thanks to the firm application of a new regime of discipline.

Stephen, at his own request, had moved to a different department, but I didn't mind that. I was beginning to see that Tom was right, they wouldn't be looking for revenge. Anyway, I was too busy during the day to be worried, and that evening, Inspector Anslow (call me Colin) came round to my house to, as he put it, put me in the picture.

'Mr Jones,' he explained, 'was far too clever for his own good. So sharp that he cut himself, to coin a cliché.'

'You don't believe they were guilty, then?' I said.

He looked at me steadily. 'I'll never forgive you if you ever repeat me,' he said.

'Cross my heart and hope to die.'

'I conducted the interviews, and I'm convinced that Miss Shenstone and Dr Wall are quite innocent of anything. Dr Enfield, I wasn't so sure about.'

'What about the patients?'

'There were grounds for suspicion, yes, but that was all. We were never anywhere near proof.' He sighed. 'I have to say it, it was a completely botched operation. Amateur. But that's what Mr Jones is, an amateur.'

I tried not to think what his reaction would be if he heard that. 'He was in the police once himself,' I told Colin.

'And you can understand why he isn't any longer. Anyway, Jo, this case is over and done with. *Finito.*'

And although he'd been unfair to Tom, when he left, he took the ghosts with him. And I knew it wouldn't be long before I heard from him again.

The next day, Stephen tried to stop me in the main corridor outside the ward. Innocent or not, I couldn't bear the sight, sound or smell of him and told him so.

'But Jo, you don't understand —'

'But I do, Stephen, only too well. Leave me alone. Dr Cannock . . .' I called out as he passed us on his way into the Path lab.

'Yes, Sister?'

Seeing him had reminded me why I'd come out.

'I was just on my way to the laboratory. These results you've sent us' — I showed him the request forms — 'I don't understand them. This one for instance . . .' On the edge of my vision, I saw Stephen slinking away . . .

Dr Cannock took the forms from me and gave a short laugh.

'I'm not surprised you don't understand them,' he said, 'the analyser has obviously caught a bug. That's not uncommon in itself, but these results should never have been released. I'll knock a few heads together for —'

'Dr Cannock' — his secretary had come out of the laboratory — 'it's Dr Enfield on the phone for you. He says it's urgent.'

Her voice died away to an echo as Dr Cannock and I gazed into each other's eyes, into each other's minds.

'It was you,' I whispered at last. I didn't hear myself, just felt my lips moving.

'Tell him I'll be along,' he called to his secretary, who didn't seem to have noticed anything.

In a flash, I saw everything.

Susan had been in his employ, it was he, not Stephen, who'd spotted what she'd been doing, perhaps while she was searching the patient files in the computer for non-believers . . .

He'd been on the working party that set up the computer system — and the flag that showed when someone was using a password they shouldn't . . . That's how he'd spotted her, using a lab worker's password while they were away; also the program she'd used, and the time of day she'd used it.

It was he who was in collusion with Enfield — maybe it had happened as Tom suggested — Enfield directing organs to the paying donees as they became available naturally . . . Cannock remarking one day: *Old Bloggs here has got the right tissue type, pity he couldn't die* . . . and then spotting Susan.

Cannock, who because of their joint research, would know as well as Miss Shenstone the tissue types of the patients, pick the ones required and then, using Mary's password, alter their notes for Susan to find.

Tom had been wrong that Sunday at the cathedral: the third lady was a man . . .

He said quietly to me: 'You could never prove anything, Sister. Never.'

I stared at him, transfixed . . .

He said: 'If you try, I swear I'll have you killed, like Susan. If you keep quiet, I promise I won't harm you. There's no reason for me to harm you. Think about it.' He strode away to the lab entrance.

'Are you all right, Jo?' Mary, touching my shoulder . . . 'You look as though you've seen a ghost.'

'I think perhaps I have . . .' I shook my head and pulled myself together. 'I don't feel so good, to tell you the truth.'

'I'm not surprised, after what you've been through.

You shouldn't have come back so quickly. Come on, lean on me.'

'No, it's all right. I'll be OK.'

I struggled on for another hour, then gave up and went home. The break-in indicator on the door was still in place. Inside, the whisky bottle beckoned, but I resisted. Lit up instead.

Then I rang the number Tom had given me.

'Tom, it's Jo,' I said when he came on the line.

'What's happened?' He'd caught the panic in my voice.

'It was C-C-Cannock,' I stuttered.

'Cannock?'

'Yes.' Now it was out, I could tell him the rest of it.

'Oh, my God,' he said tiredly, when I'd finished. 'I've been so stupid . . . Mary Tamworth — why didn't Cannock notice her password was being abused? Answer — because he was doing it himself.'

'Can we do anything about it? Won't the police . . .?'

'I don't know. They aren't going to want to reopen it after the last fiasco.'

'Then he was right,' I said dully. 'There's no way of proving it. Tom, *what . . . am . . . I . . . going . . . to . . . do . . .?*'

'He's not going to do anything, Jo, not yet. Probably never.'

'Probably isn't good enough. He could decide at any time that I'm too great a risk and —'

'Perhaps we'd better get you away from there.'

'And it could never be proved . . .'

'Jo, try not to panic. Let me think. Jo, I swear he isn't going to harm you. Let me think about it . . .'

He rang off to do his thinking.

I succumbed to the whisky bottle and did some thinking of my own.

He had me. He could arrange my demise, go abroad on holiday or something and nothing could ever be proved, even if I did leave a 'To be opened in the event of my death' note.

Even with Tom's knowing . . .

Colin . . .?

But what would he think if I told him? And in the unlikely event he believed me, what could he do?

I'd have to leave the area. Change my name.

And wonder for the rest of my life when the sword would fall . . .

And why *should* I leave Latchvale, my parents, my home . . .?

My little house, so recently exorcized of its ghosts . . . Why *should* I?

Chapter 25

West Midlands *Morning Post*

LATCHVALE PATHOLOGIST KILLED IN CAR EXPLOSION.

Police 'cannot rule out terrorist attack'.

Dr John Cannock, Medical Director of Pathology at St Chad's hospital, was killed in Latchvale yesterday afternoon when his Jaguar XJS exploded outside St Chad's cathedral. No one else was hurt, although the cathedral sustained slight structural damage. Superintendent Rayment of the West Midlands Constabulary told the *Morning Post*: 'We are quite certain that this explosion was caused by a bomb, although we don't know yet whether it was detonated manually or by a timing device. Unless and until we are able to discover a motive for the killing of Dr Cannock, we cannot rule out a terrorist attack, especially in view of the similar killing of a transplant consultant in London earlier today. This would not be the first time that eminent doctors have been targeted by terrorists.'

An eyewitness, Mr Leonard Sutton, who was knocked from his feet by the blast, described it as: 'Like the door of a furnace opening. It must have been appalling for the poor bloke inside.'

Mr Sutton did not require medical treatment.

If you enjoyed *Sisters of Mercy* you might be
interested in *Death Before Time* by Andrew Puckett,
also published by Endeavour Press.

**Extract from *Death Before Time*
by Andrew Puckett**

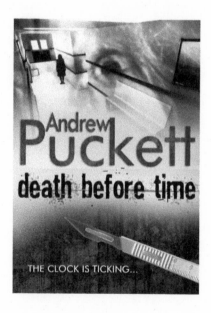

Chapter 1

As Fraser gazed down at the old man's body, tiny as a London sparrow beneath the hospital sheets, he was swept by a wave of desolation, and then by a fury so intense that he could feel the blood pricking at his eyeballs . . .

Pneumonia – *again*. They were wrong – *again* . . .

"'Scuse me, Doc –" Wally the Trolley, the mortuary technician, come to collect the body.

He turned and walked quickly away, out of the brightly lit ward, out of the hospital. He found a bench, sat down and breathed deeply as the breeze rustled the leaves of the young tree beside it.

Somebody had deliberately killed the old man. Not just let him die, but quite deliberately put him to death, murdered him. And he was not the first. All the others, they'd been murdered too and now he, Dr Fraser Callan, was going to have to do something about it.

But what? Tell someone? Philip? He wouldn't believe it. The police? They'd ask a lot of questions, find nothing and leave him to stew in the resulting acrimony.

It came to him that there was only one thing he could do. He didn't like it, but he'd have to.

He stayed there on the bench until he'd calmed down enough to control himself, then went back inside, hoping that no one had noticed him. He went to his room, shut the door and looked up the old man's medical record on the computer.

Friday: Chest infection, put on ampicillin . . . Saturday: Stable . . . Sunday: Developed into pneumonia, erythromycin added . . .

But too late, all too late. He'd died early this morning.

He sat back in his chair and thought, his mind icy calm now.

To know that murder had been done wasn't enough, you had to be able to prove it, or at least show evidence for it.

Aye, gey and easy – when he hadn't the least idea who was doing it, never mind how it was being done . . .

Figures. It would come down to figures.

He spent the next two days gathering them, and then keyed in the phone number he'd never thought to need again. If Marcus was surprised to hear from him, he didn't show it and told him to come up the day after tomorrow, Friday.

He begged the day off from Edwina, saying his sick

mother needed him again, and caught the early train to London on Friday morning.

As the fields of Wilts and Berks slid by, he thought about Marcus, and Tom . . .

Marcus Evans was a civil servant with a difference. He ran a small section in the Department of Health whose purpose was to investigate allegations, or even rumours, of wrongdoing in the NHS that couldn't be looked into in any other way. Not many people knew about it. Fraser only did because he'd been on the receiving end of its attentions the year before.

He was shown into Marcus' office in Whitehall at 9.30. Tom was there as well. They both stood and Marcus came across and shook hands.

"Fraser, come and sit down. Would you like some coffee?"

"Aye, I would please."

As Marcus busied himself pouring it, Fraser glanced round the room . . . It somehow managed to be both light and formal at the same time, the lightness accentuated by the cream carpet and pale walls, the formality by the dark furnishings and prints of old London.

"Before anything else," Marcus said as he handed him a cup and saucer, "May I say how sorry we were to hear about your wife." Tom nodded and murmured his agreement.

Fraser had to clear his throat before he could reply. "Thanks."

Frances had died six months earlier of leukaemia. He knew they'd both been at the funeral, but they'd left without speaking to him.

"Now, how can we help you?" Marcus said.

No point in pussy-footing around it . . . "I've been working as a locum staff grade at a hospital for older people in Wansborough for the last couple of months, and I think . . ." he broke off, then continued, "I know fine well that someone's systematically bumping them off." His accent, noticeably Glaswegian, became more pronounced as he finished.

In the silence that followed, the curious thought went through his head that Marcus had been held in a time machine since he'd last seen him; he seemed to be wearing exactly the same dark suit and tie, with the same shine to the bald dome of his head above the heavy walrus moustache.

"I see," Marcus said at last. "You say you *know* – d'you mean you have evidence?" He spoke softly as always, with a faint London twang to his voice.

"Statistical evidence," Fraser said.

"You know what they say about statistics?" said Tom, speaking for the first time. He hadn't changed much either, Fraser thought – leather jacketed, sharp featured and hard – and there was nothing faint about his London accent.

"Lies and damned lies, you mean? I've no reason for either."

Tom didn't reply and he continued, "I've compared the death rate at Wansborough with other community hospitals and it's higher, significantly higher." He reached down to undo his briefcase. "If you'll just take a look . . ."

"We'll look at your figures in a minute," said Marcus. "You say patients are being killed – any patients, or a particular type or category?"

"Aye. Those whose lives some might say were not worth living."

"That's subjective, to say the least."

"I don't mean vegetative cases being allowed to die naturally – that happens, of course – I mean mentally alert people with two or three or more months left to live being deliberately killed."

"So you're talking about involuntary euthanasia."

"I am."

"How's it being done?"

"I don't know. I only know that it *is* being done, and that it's being made to look natural. The one's I've noticed seem to be dying of pneumonia."

"Any idea who's doing it?" Tom again.

"No, I don't know that, either."

Marcus regarded him for a moment . . .

Fraser *had* changed; even with his beard, he could see that his face was thinner, darker, the dark brown eyes deeper in their sockets, giving him a mien even more intense than before. "Perhaps you'd better tell us from the beginning," he said. "How did you come to be working there? It's not really your line, is it?"

"No," Fraser agreed. He began haltingly: "After Frances died, I didna know what I wanted to do . . ."

*

Although he'd been expecting it, even almost willing it at times, her death had shaken him more than he could have imagined.

He'd been formally cleared of any wrongdoing and was thus officially available for work again. Unofficially however, his erstwhile colleagues still blamed him for their misfortunes and let him know that his return would be deemed "inappropriate". They'd offered him three months pay while he looked for another job and, dazed by grief, he'd accepted . . .

"You should never have agreed to that," said Marcus.

"You were shafted," said Tom.

"Aye, I know that – *now*," Fraser said . . .

He tried to lose himself walking over Dartmoor and Exmoor. He dreamed strange dreams in which Frances spoke to him, then woke up crying because he couldn't remember what she'd said. Guilt rode him like a vulture: he was alive, she was dead, it was his fault and he had to atone in some way. Which is why he'd volunteered to go and work in Africa for a year for a charity.

It hadn't worked.

It wasn't the heat, or the flies or the disease, and he

liked the people, whom he thought the happiest he'd ever met, despite their poverty. What he couldn't stand was the corruption of some of the indigenous petty officials and one day, he'd told one of them exactly what he thought of him.

It hadn't been well received and his head was the price of peace.

"I told you so," Mary, his mother in law, said when he got back. She had, too. "So what are you going to do now?"

"I don't know," he confessed.

Fortunately, his house had only been let on a short lease and was empty, but he needed money to pay the mortgage.

She said, "Wait there a minute." She left the room, came back a few minutes later with a sheaf of newspaper cuttings. "I've been meaning to show you these for a long time, but then what with Frances and everything else . . . " She tailed off . . ."Anyway, look at them now while I make some tea."

It was a series of articles, mostly from the Telegraph, on the state of care for older people in NHS hospitals. There were case studies of elderly, but relatively healthy people going into hospital for trivial complains, then dying from the treatment they received there. Being found by relatives in urine-soaked bedclothes that hadn't been changed for days. Food put out of reach so that they couldn't eat, bedsores you could put your fist into, instructions such as *Not For Resuscitation* and *Nil By Mouth* surreptitiously attached to their notes.

"If you want to help suffering humanity," Mary said, "why don't you go and work in one of those places?"

He looked at her. "I do remember hearing about this, but I thought they'd sorted it out now . . ."

"I thought so too, but then last week, I saw this –" She handed him another cutting.

The headline was *Why did Mabel have to die like this*? Mabel Fisher, a healthy woman in her seventies, had gone into hospital for a minor operation and died there from malnutrition. This was followed by a report from the charity Age Alert claiming that six out of ten older patients in hospital were at risk of malnutrition and dehydration because the nursing staff were simply too busy to feed them properly. This meant that not only were they taking longer to get better and thus exacerbating the bed shortage, but some, like Mabel, were actually dying.

"Six out of ten," he repeated to himself . . . "I knew there was a nursing shortage, but I never thought it was that bad."

"Well, why don't you go and find out for yourself?"

So, a couple of days later, when he saw the advert for a locum staff grade to cover maternity leave at Wansborough Community Hospital in Wilts, he rang the consultant in change, Dr Armitage, and arranged to go and see him the following afternoon.

Philip Armitage was a smallish man of about fifty with sandy hair, a goatee and mild grey eyes behind glasses.

"I'll show you round, then we'll have a talk," he said. He was gently spoken with a faint Midlands accent.

The hospital, which was in the grounds of the Royal Infirmary, was in the form of a misshapen T, with beds in the long stroke and admin in the short. It looked as though it had been built that way to fit into a left over piece of land (which he found later was the case). It appeared very cramped from the outside, and yet inside seemed airy and spacious – a bit like an NHS Tardis, Fraser thought with a smile.

"How many patients?" he asked.

"Forty-five altogether, thirty women and fifteen men."

It was freshly painted in blue and yellow, clean, well equipped and, so far was he could see, well run. There was also very little smell.

Many of the old hospital wards he remembered, especially those for older patients, had held what he'd thought of as the miasma of the infirm. It's a smell that hits you straight between the nostrils and when you stop noticing it, then it's time to worry, because it's impregnated your clothes.

Fraser commented on it.

"Having a new purpose-built unit helps of course," Armitage told him. "Although good nursing and cleaning staff may have something to do with it."

They walked back to his office. "Not quite what you were expecting?" he enquired of Fraser with a twinkle.

Fraser had to admit that it wasn't.

"Perhaps you shouldn't believe everything you read in the papers." His steady gaze and faint smile seemed to be mocking him.

"Perhaps not," Fraser agreed, reluctantly smiling.

"Oh, I know there were some places that were frankly vile," Armitage continued, serious now, "This hospital replaced one of them in fact. There are still some which – er – leave something to be desired, shall we say? But this isn't one of them."

"Obviously not," Fraser said.

There was a knock on the door and a secretary brought in some tea. While Armitage poured, he glanced round the room. It was austere almost to the point of starkness – no photos, no pictures or plants. The only thing of interest was a bookcase that seemed to contain old medical books and Fraser wondered if he was a collector –

"Sugar?"

"Oh – no thanks."

He handed Fraser his tea and then questioned him about his medical experience. He asked him why he wanted the job.

"The truth is," Fraser said, "I'm not sure what I want to do with my career at the moment." He told him briefly and unemotionally about Frances.

"My dear man, I'm so sorry."

Fraser couldn't remember the last time he'd been called that, yet there was no doubting Armitage's sincerity.

"Thank you." He paused. "I need time, but I also need some money."

"I can understand that." He regarded Fraser for a moment. "I think you're the right person for this post."

Fraser looked at him in surprise. "You're offering it to me?"

Armitage nodded. "Yes."

"D'you not have other people to interview?"

"Only one other person has showed any interest and I didn't think they were suitable. We were about to re advertise."

"I see . . ."

"Perhaps I should have told you earlier, there's a flat in the doctor's quarters that goes with it."

Accommodation had been one of the two things worrying Fraser. He now gave voice to the other.

"You mentioned earlier I'd be working under one of your Associate Specialists, could I meet him – or her?"

"I was about to suggest that," Armitage said, standing up, "And it *is* a her – Edwina Tate."

He took him a little way along the corridor to an open door. The woman working at the VDU swivelled round in her chair and stood up. She was tall and slim, a bit younger than Armitage, with a thin face and long dark hair shot with grey.

"Hello." She held out a soft hand, then at Armitage's prompting, outlined what she wanted. She had a somehow otherworldly manner and Fraser neither liked nor disliked her. He felt he could work with her.

As they left, Armitage said, "While you're here, you'd better meet Ranjid, our other Associate Specialist and also my deputy."

He tapped on another door, marked Dr R Singh, and pushed it open.

"Oh – I'm sorry Ranjid, you're busy."

He quickly pulled the door shut and they moved on.

"So you'll think about it and let me know?" he said to Fraser as they returned to his office.

"I'll do that," said Fraser.

"Tomorrow? I'm sorry to push you, but if you don't want it, we're going to have to look for someone else."

"Of course," Fraser said. "Tomorrow."

He had thought about it as the MG roared throatily back along the motorway to Bristol. Wansborough itself was possibly the most unappealing town he'd seen in his life, viciously ugly office blocks and windswept car parks and shopping malls, but he'd rather liked Armitage and felt he could rub along with Edwina.

He also thought about the scene he'd witnessed in the second before Armitage had pulled the door shut – two faces, the one behind the desk clearly Asian with good looking, regular features now twisted in anger, the other swivelled round towards them, startlingly beautiful, the beauty accentuated by the flush over the high cheek bones and the twin tear trails . . .

As Armitage had observed, they'd been busy – a new variant of *doctors and nurses*, perhaps?

Was it any concern of his? No. The Asian was obviously Dr R Singh, but he wouldn't be working with him . . .

Besides, he'd thought, it was only for four months.

ENDEAVOUR INK

Endeavour Ink is an imprint of Endeavour Press.

If you enjoyed *Sisters of Mercy* check out
Endeavour Press's eBooks here:
www.endeavourpress.com

For weekly updates on our free and discounted eBooks sign up
to our newsletter:
www.endeavourpress.com

Follow us on Twitter:
@EndeavourPress